Middleton Public Library
7425 Hubbard Avenue
Middleton, WI 53562

All-of-a-kind Family

Sydney Taylor

ILLUSTRATIONS BY Helen John

A Yearling Book

Published by
Dell Yearling
an imprint of
Random House Children's Books
1540 Broadway
New York, New York 10036

Visit us on the Web! www.randomhouse.com/kids

Educators and librarians, for a variety of teaching tools, visit us at www.randomhouse.com/teachers

ISBN: 0-440-40059-7

Printed in the United States of America

Two Previous Editions

January 1989

60 59 58 57 56 55

OPM

To my mother and father who made it possible;

To my husband who made it probable.

All-of-a-kind Family

The Library Lady

"THAT SLOWPOKE SARAH!" Henny cried. "She's making us late!"

Mama's girls were going to the library, and Henny was impatient.

"If it was Charlotte, I could understand," said Ella, who was the eldest and very serious. "I'd know Charlotte was off dreaming in some corner. But what can be keeping Sarah?"

"All the best books will be gone," complained Henny. "Maybe she forgot it's Friday."

"No!" interrupted Charlotte. "Not Sarah!"

No, not Sarah, nor any of the girls could forget that Friday was library day.

Almost no East Side child owned a book when Mama's children were little girls. That was an unheard-of luxury. It was heavenly enough to be able to borrow books from the public library and that was where the children always went on Friday afternoons. Right after school, they rushed off happily to get fresh reading material for the week end. Even Gertie who was not yet old enough to "belong" took the weekly trip to look at the picture magazines.

Where *was* Sarah? Mama was beginning to be concerned too. It wasn't like the child to be late.

At last footsteps could be heard on the creaky back steps. Henny ran to open the kitchen door and poked her head out. "Here she comes," she called.

"Well, it's about time," said Ella. "Come on, let's get our books."

Henny opened the door wider. "What's the matter?" her sisters heard her asking.

A woebegone little figure, face streaked with tears, walked slowly into the kitchen.

"Mama," piped up Gertie, "Sarah's crying."

"Sarah, what's the matter? What's happened?"

Sarah didn't answer. Walking over to the hard brown

leather couch, she threw herself face downward, weeping bitterly. Her sisters gathered in a little group around her.

Mama came over and sat down beside Sarah. Gently she stroked her hair and let the child weep. After a while she said softly, "Sarah, tell us what happened."

Between sobs, the muffled words came slowly, "My — library book — is — lost."

Lost! The children looked at each other in dismay. Such a thing had never happened in the family before. "Ooh — how awful!" Ella said, and then was sorry that the words had escaped her for they seemed to bring on a fresh burst of tears.

"Now, now, stop crying, Sarah," Mama said. "You'll only make yourself sick. Come, we'll wash your face and then you'll tell us all about it."

Obediently Sarah followed Mama to the kitchen sink.

"Does it mean we can't go to the library, ever again?" Charlotte whispered to Ella.

Ella shook her head. "I don't think so."

"Maybe we could change over to another branch," suggested Henny.

The cold water felt good on Sarah's flushed face. She was quiet now and could talk.

"It wasn't really me that lost the book. It was my friend, Tillie. You know how Tillie never takes a book out herself, but she's always wanting to read mine. When I told her about *Peter and Polly In Winter,* she begged me to lend it to her. She promised she'd give it back to me on Friday.

"When I asked her for it today, she said that she put it in my desk yesterday, but Mama, she didn't! She really didn't!"

"Are you sure?" asked Mama. "Maybe you left it in school."

"I looked a thousand times. That's why I came so late. I kept hunting and hunting all over the schoolroom."

"Maybe you brought it home with you yesterday and left it here in the house."

"Then it should be on the shelf under the whatnot," Ella said.

Hopefully, everybody rushed over to the whatnot where the library books were kept, but alas, there was no Peter and Polly book there today.

"I cleaned the house pretty thoroughly this morning," said Mama. "I don't remember seeing the book anywhere. But let's all look again anyway."

How anxiously everyone searched. The children peered into every corner of the two bedrooms and they poked under beds and dressers. No one believed it was in the front room, but still they searched it diligently. They searched and searched until they had to agree that it was useless to continue.

When they were back in the kitchen again, Sarah said tearfully, "How can I go and tell the library that the book is lost?" She was ready to cry again.

"I'm afraid they won't let you take out any more books until we pay for this one," Mama worried. "And a book costs a lot of money."

"But Tillie lost the book," argued Sarah. "She should pay."

"We can't be sure of that," Mama said. "Tillie claims she returned it. Maybe someone else took it."

"No library could make me pay for any old book." Henny was just trying to cover up how bad she felt too.

"I'm afraid the library will expect you to pay for it. And it's only right," continued Mama. "You borrowed the book and that makes you responsible. The library lets you borrow the book and you're not supposed to lend it to anybody else. I know you wanted to be kind to Tillie, but if Tillie wants to read a library book, then she should take out her own. I wish I could help you pay for this, but you know, Sarah, there's no money for such things."

"But Mama, will you come with me and talk to the library lady?"

Mama shook her head. "No, Sarah, that's something you must do yourself. If you explain just how it happened, I'm sure the library lady will understand that you didn't mean to be careless. Find out what you have to do, and we'll talk about it when you get back. Now you'll all have to hurry. There's not much time left before supper. So, the rest of you, see if you can choose your books quickly today."

Mama had said to hurry but Sarah's feet wouldn't walk. They felt like lead. In her chest was a lump of lead too. Ella put her arm around Sarah's shoulder. Even Gertie forsook her idol Charlotte and came over to Sarah. She slipped her little hand into Sarah's, her brown eyes large in sympathy.

A branch of the New York Public Library was only a few blocks from their home; soon the familiar brown building came into view. Through the high door and up the staircase they went. With each step, Sarah grew more despairing. They'll take my card away, she thought. I just know they will. I'll never be able to take out any more books.

Once inside the room, Sarah hung back, fearing to join the line at the "in" desk. She looked back down the staircase

16

longingly. It would be so easy to run down the stairs and out into the street and just never come back.

"Come on, Sarah," Ella said. "Let's get it over with." Gently she pulled Sarah towards the desk and the five children fell in line.

Henny nudged Sarah. "Look," she said, "isn't that a new library lady? She's pretty!" she added.

Sarah studied the new library lady anxiously. She looked so fresh and clean in a crisp white shirtwaist with long sleeves ending in paper cuffs pinned tightly at the wrists. Her hair is light, just like mine, Sarah said to herself. And she has such little ears. I think she has a kind face. She watched as the librarian's slender fingers pulled the cards in and out of the index file. How does she keep her nails so clean, Sarah wondered, thinking of her own scrubby ones.

It was Ella's turn to have her book stamped. The library lady looked up and Sarah could see the deep blue of her eyes. The library lady smiled.

She has dimples, Sarah thought. Surely a lady with dimples could never be harsh.

The smile on the library lady's face deepened. In front of her desk stood five little girls dressed exactly alike.

"My goodness! Are you all one family?"

"Yes, all one family," Henny spoke up. "I'm Henrietta, Henny for short; I'm ten. Ella's twelve, Sarah is eight, Charlotte is six, and Gertie is four."

"A steps-and-stairs family!" The library lady laughed and the tiny freckles on her pert nose seemed to laugh with her.

"That's a good name for us," Ella said. "Some people call us an all-of-a-kind family."

"All of a very nice kind," smiled the library lady. "And you have such nice names! I'm Miss Allen, your new librarian. I'm very glad to meet you."

Her eyes travelled over the five little girls. Such sad-looking faces. Not a smile among them.

"Better tell the teacher what happened," Charlotte whispered to Sarah.

"She's not a teacher, silly. She's a library lady." Henny's scornful reply was loud enough for Miss Allen to hear. The dimples began to show again.

Sarah stepped forward. "Library lady," she began, twisting and untwisting the fingers of her hands.

Miss Allen looked at Sarah and suddenly noticed the red-rimmed eyes and the nose all swollen from weeping. Something was wrong. No wonder the faces were so unhappy.

"Let me see, now. Which one are you?" she asked.

"Sarah," the little girl replied and the tears began to swim in her eyes.

The library lady put her hand under the little girl's chin and lifted it up. "Now, now, Sarah. Nothing can be that bad."

Sarah said tearfully, "Yes, it can. I — I —" She couldn't go on.

"Here." Ella put a handkerchief to her sister's nose.

Miss Allen went on speaking as if she did not notice anything unusual. "Did you enjoy your book?"

Sarah's voice broke. "I loved it. But nobody else will ever be able to read it again . . ."

"She means she lost it!" Henny blurted out.

"She didn't lose it. It was Tillie." Charlotte rushed to Sarah's defense.

"Oh, I'm so sorry," said the library lady, looking bewilderedly from one to the other. "Who is Tillie?"

Thereupon Ella unfolded the whole story and the library lady listened sympathetically.

"Mama says I must pay for the book and I'm going to — every cent." Sarah was trembling. "But I don't have enough money now."

"How much will she have to pay?" Ella asked.

"I'll have to look it up in the catalogue," Miss Allen answered. She pulled out a big book and began to look through its pages. It really was a shame that this had happened. She knew that the people who lived on the East Side had to count their pennies carefully. Even a small sum would seem like a fortune to these children.

Her heart went out to the little group. How sincere they were and how anxious to do the right thing. She wished that she could pay for the book herself. But she could not risk hurting either the children or their parents by making the offer.

She made her voice as cheerful as she could. "Well, it's not nearly as bad as I thought. Let's see now. Do you have any spending money, Sarah?"

"A penny a day . . . and I can save my pennies. I don't care for candy anyway." She added quickly, "I have seventeen cents saved up in my penny bank."

Seventeen cents! thought the library lady. How can I tell her that the book costs a dollar? "Is that all you have?"

Sarah nodded shyly. "Yes."

"She was going to buy a doll." Gertie's voice filled the silence. "A doll with real hair."

The library lady looked at the sad little figure for a moment.

"Sarah," she said, "the book costs a dollar. If you pay the seventeen cents the next time you come, you will owe eighty-three cents. After that, I will make a special arrangement so you can pay one penny each week. I know it will take a very long time to pay the whole amount but you can save for your doll at the same time."

Sarah's eyes opened wide in unbelief. "You mean, I can save for my doll and still pay for the book?"

"That's right," said the library lady, and they both smiled.

Meanwhile the other children were whispering among themselves. Finally Ella spoke up. "Could we help pay? Each of us can bring a penny every week. We've collected three cents right now."

Henny said shamefacedly, "I already spent my penny today but I promise I'll bring it next week like the others."

"That's a wonderful idea! Sarah must be very proud to have such thoughtful sisters."

Sarah was proud. She gave them each a hug. "And when I get my doll, you can all play with her."

"Isn't it nice to have a family to share your troubles?" asked the library lady.

"Have you any sisters?" Sarah asked shyly.

"No, dear. Nor brothers. I'm the only one."

"Isn't that lonesome?" Charlotte asked. The children all felt sorry for the library lady now.

"Yes, dear, it is lonesome. But come now, aren't you going to take out any books today?"

"Can Sarah take out a book too?" questioned Henny.

"Yes, she can, so long as you'll be paying for the lost book."

Sarah clasped her hands together joyfully. "Oh, thank you! I think you're the nicest, kindest library lady in the whole world."

Miss Allen's smile was warm and friendly. "Run along now, dear, and get your book."

As she worked, Miss Allen found herself watching the five little girls. How quaint they were in their stiffly starched white aprons over dark woolen dresses. They looked for all the world like wide-open umbrellas.

Had she been able to peek under those dresses, she would have understood why they billowed out in such a manner. Underneath were *three* petticoats, a woolly, flannel one first, a simple cotton one next, with both of these topped by a fancy muslin garment which was starched to a scratchy crispness. In order to save money, Mama made those petticoats herself. Still further underneath was long woolen underwear, over which were pulled heavy knitted woolen stockings, making thin legs look like well-stuffed frankfurters. How the girls hated those stockings! They itched so! *And they never wore out!* Mama knitted them herself on long needles and she could always reknit the holes the children made.

Miss Allen could see that the stockings were bothering Sarah. She looked very comical as she kept rubbing one leg against the other. Clutching her new book tightly to her, she made her way back to the desk.

"Come on, everybody. It's late," Ella warned.

The children quickly chose their books and gave them to the library lady for stamping.

They raced home on happy feet. They couldn't wait to tell Mama that their beloved Friday afternoons at the library were not going to be spoiled after all.

Dusting Is Fun

AFTER BREAKFAST Monday morning, Mama said, "Henny, put aside your book. It's your turn to dust the front room today."

"Mama, let Ella do it," Henny said. "I have to finish my homework."

"I will not," retorted Ella, her black eyes snapping. "It's your turn. I did it yesterday."

"Ella is right," Mama said. "You should have done your homework yesterday instead of leaving it until the last moment. You'll have to do it."

"Then let Charlotte do it. She hasn't done a thing all morning. I've got to finish my homework."

"Charlotte will help dry the breakfast dishes this morning.

That's her job today. Your job today is to dust the front room."

"All right, then. I'll have a swell excuse when the teacher asks me why I haven't finished my homework. I'll say my mother took up all my time with dusting." Henny tossed her blonde curls defiantly. How her sisters envied her those curls!

She slammed the front-room door as she went in to perform her job. Mama knew it would be a job badly done. She sighed. She was tired of the girls forever trying to avoid doing this chore. She would have to think of something.

After the children had gone to school, Mama thought. Frequently she smiled. She got out her sewing box and began rummaging in it, picking out a dozen colored buttons. Then she put the box away and went back to her work, humming softly to herself.

The following morning Mama put the buttons in her apron pocket and went into the front room, closing the door. The children stared after her and then looked at one another.

"Say, do you think Mama is going to dust the front room herself this morning?" Henny asked.

"She didn't have a dust rag with her," Ella said.

"Maybe she's looking around to see how dusty the room is," came from Charlotte.

Mama was in the front room for a few minutes. When she came out, she was smiling.

"Well, girls," she said, "we're going to play a game and I've been getting the room ready for it."

The children became very interested. "What game?"

"It's a game of hide-and-seek," Mama answered. "I have hidden a dozen buttons in the front room. If the one who dusts can find those twelve buttons, she will have done a wonderful dusting job, and I won't even have to check up on her. Now let's see, whose turn is it to dust today?"

"It's my turn, my turn!" shouted Sarah.

"Aw, Ma! Let me do it today!"

"No, me!"

The children fought for a chance at the hated chore. Even baby Gertie who had never been expected to do so before, now was eager to try her hand at it.

"It's really Sarah's turn," Mama said. "So in you go, Sarah. I expect you to bring back twelve buttons."

Sarah took up the dustcloth and fairly skipped out of the kitchen. In a minute she was back again. "Forgot the stool," she explained. Eight-year-old Sarah was still too small to reach the high places without the aid of a stool. Now fully armed with dustcloth and stool, she disappeared into the front room, while her sisters watched enviously.

"You needn't be so unhappy," Mama told them. "You'll each get your turn at the game when your dusting day comes."

Sarah stood still beside the closed door of the front room and looked about her. Such a big room, she thought. So many good hiding places in all its furnishings. What would be the best way to hunt?

I guess I'd better dust the same way I always do, she finally decided, and proceeded towards the big table standing in the middle of the room. She removed the fruit bowl that was set in the exact center of the table. She dusted the big family album that rested at one end. No time today to examine the pictures of a youthful Papa and Mama without any children. Today she had to hunt for buttons, so she put the album on a chair without even opening it. Then she removed the tablecloth. No button here. She got down on the thick red-and-green carpet to dust the table leg. At the base of the leg staring up at her lay a shiny red button. Sarah's eyes began to dance with excitement. This was going to be fun! Button number one was slipped into her apron pocket.

The table was finished and cover and objects replaced. Chairs were carefully dusted next. They were hard to do, and Mama had five of them. The first yielded nothing. Neither did the second. The third had a button slid in neatly in one of the hard-to-dust places in its back. Button number two hit button number one with a click as it was deposited in Sarah's apron pocket.

The last two chairs were dusted but no more buttons turned up. Sarah stood on the stool to dust off the top of the upright piano. She dusted off each knickknack thoroughly, and hopefully lifted the piano cover so that she might wipe the wood smooth of dirt. Her effort was rewarded, for there lying peacefully on the piano top was button number three.

Now Sarah was tempted to give up cleaning the rest of the piano. There was so much to it and surely Mama wouldn't put two buttons in one piece of furniture. Still it wouldn't be playing the game fair and, besides, one never could tell. Mama might be trying to catch her in just such a trick. Sarah dusted the foot pedals, but found no buttons. Nor were there any on the lid covering the keyboard. Piano keys had to be kept clean, too, so up went the lid. And there was another button!

Sarah was jubilant. She carried the stool over to the mantel shelf. Up she went, dustcloth tight in one hand. Now she could lift the china shepherd and shepherdess. She liked to handle these, especially the shepherdess, so dainty in her pink-and-blue dress with tiny rosebuds on it. She picked her up first. Something rattled! In the opening at the back of the little lady, which was for flowers, Mama had put button number five. And that was all Sarah found on the mantel shelf.

Two small round tables stood in front of the lace-curtained windows. Sarah started to work on these. On the first she discovered nothing, but under the doily which decorated the top of the second table, she found the sixth button.

Mama wanted her helpers to dust window sills. Sarah remembered and because she did, she was able to add both the seventh and eighth buttons to her apron pocket. Sitting right on the floor near the white window woodwork was button number nine. If Sarah had neglected the woodwork, she never would have found it.

She stopped in front of the tall mirror that stood between the windows, and began making faces at herself. "Now where shall I hunt for three more buttons?" she asked her reflection.

As she looked about, Sarah's eyes fell on the colored calendar that Mama had hung on the wall. This is a new month, she thought. I might as well change the calendar while I'm here. Neatly Sarah tore off the sheet that said November, 1912.

She got down on the rug and looked about the room thoughtfully. Pretty nearly everything had been gone over, excepting the large sea shells lying on the floor on each side of the mirror. Sarah liked these shells. If she held one close to her ear, she could hear a strange noise like the roaring of waves. She picked up a shell, dusted it off, and held it close to her ear for a minute, listening. She hoped a button would pop out, but there was no button, only the same rushing sound. Sarah picked up the second shell and a button looked up at her. Ten buttons found — only two more to go.

All that was left was the woodwork. Sarah dusted the door first, for the ridge near the bottom was such a dust-gathering place. And right there on the flooring below the door ridge was button number eleven!

The baseboards about the entire room were dusted, but there was still one button missing. That meant Sarah had overlooked something, but what? Had she dusted the underneath part of the second table or had she forgotten to do it in the excitement of finding the button under the doily? Well, she'd do it again just to make sure. She was very glad indeed that she did make sure for there on the table's curved-up leg reposed button number twelve!

She threw open the front-room door and came running into the kitchen, crying out joyfully: "I found them! I found them all, every single one of them! Ma, you certainly picked some swell hiding places! But it was fun. I'd like to do it again!"

For the next week Mama had a beautifully clean front room and there was not a single grumble.

After that the children might have tired of the game and Mama would have been right back where she started. But she was a wise mother. At the end of the week, the buttons went back into the sewing box. Mama said she didn't have time to put the buttons out every morning. From now on, they would be hidden only occasionally. No child would know just when she might find buttons during her dusting because Mama would hide the buttons at night after the girls had gone to sleep. Also the number would be different, sometimes six, sometimes ten.

Mama was as good as her word. Sometimes she brought out her buttons once or twice during the week. Sometimes she would let two weeks pass by without producing them. And then every day in one memorable week, Mama hid buttons *plus* one shiny copper penny. "Finders-keepers," she told the little dusters.

The grumbling didn't stop completely, but it was not nearly so loud or so often. And in the meantime, the children were taught to be the best little housekeepers in the whole world.

Rainy Day Surprise

THE EAST SIDE was not pretty. There was no grass. Grass couldn't very well grow on slate sidewalks or in cobble-stoned gutters. There were no flowers except those one saw in the shops of the few florists. There were no tall trees lining the streets. There were tall gas lampposts instead. There was no running brook in which children might splash on hot summer days. But there was the East River. Its waters stretched out wide and darkly green, and it smelt of fish, ships, and garbage.

Like many other families, Mama and Papa and their children lived in the crowded tenement house section of the lower East Side of New York City. But unlike most of these families, their home was a four-room apartment which occupied an entire floor in a two-storied private house.

Papa had a shop not far from the river in the basement of an old warehouse. To get into the place, the children had to climb down a dangerously narrow wooden staircase with no supporting banisters. This did not stop them from visiting Papa. They came often because they found the shop a fascinating place. It was a junk shop.

It had its own peculiar odor — damp, musty, basementy. The smell was not unpleasant. As a matter of fact, the children liked it. After descending the stairs, they came into a large open space. Here were Papa's desk and chair, where he did such bookkeeping as was necessary.

On the opposite side a few chairs formed a half-circle about a small coal stove. In the winter the little stove glowed fiery red in a vain effort to heat such a large area. On its top a teakettle sang an unceasing merry tune. Papa kept it filled all day so that the peddlers in the neighborhood might warm their insides with a hot cup of tea as they sat about and chatted. In summer, the stove was cold and there was no tea, but the lack of sunshine made the place moist and cool, so that the peddlers still sat in Papa's chairs and chatted.

Beyond the large open part, the whole shop was partitioned off neatly. First there was the metals room. In there lay a towering pile of all kinds of old iron, zinc, tin, and copper ware. Next to this was the paper section filled with stacks of old newspapers and magazines collected by the peddlers. Last of all was the rag compartment; it was there that Papa did most of his work. The rags had to be sorted; woolens from cottons, white from colored, jerseys from worsteds. After sorting they were tossed into tall, sack-lined wooden bins.

When the bins were piled high with rags, Papa climbed into them and stamped them down, for he had no mechanical press to do this for him.

Sometimes when Papa wasn't in a special hurry, he let the children take turns at sewing the bale covers for the rags. He used an enormous, curved, iron needle, threaded with strong rope and as it slipped through the sacking, it made a large round hole into which the rope would fit nicely.

Making bales offered great fun for the children, but it was not much fun for Papa, especially in the winter. There was no coal stove in this section; it would be too dangerous with so many rags lying around. Papa's fingers grew stiff with cold. He had to stop his work frequently to blow on them.

They got so badly chapped that the skin cracked. Into the cracks the dust and dirt seeped and though Papa tried hard every night to wash his hands clean and make them smooth with oil, they always remained rough and dirt-stained.

One morning, the children woke to the sound of falling rain. Charlotte pressed her nose against the window pane. "It's raining cats and dogs."

"Oh, botheration!" exclaimed Henny. "Now what're we going to do?"

"Well," suggested Ella, "why don't we go to Fanny's house for a change?" Fanny was Henny's special chum outside of the family.

"Nope, we can't. We're mad at each other."

"Again!" Sarah was amused. "You're forever mad and glad at each other. Can't you get glad just for today?"

"No, I'm not going to — ever! She's a big tattletale. I'm never going to speak to her again!"

"You'll have to make up with her when Yom Kippur (Day of Atonement) comes. You know everyone must forgive each other on that day," Ella reminded her.

"Oh, it's a long ways off to Yom Kippur." Henny shrugged

37

her shoulders. "What I want to know is, what're we going to do today?"

"You can all help me. There's plenty to do." Mama had come into the bedroom in time to answer Henny's question.

The children made long faces. Mama laughed. "Don't look so glum," she said. "There'll be plenty of time for play."

It was just as Mama said. They were finished with their household chores at ten o'clock. By eleven, those who were taking piano lessons had their turn at the piano for a twenty-minute practice period. After that they were free.

"We could play acting," suggested Henny. "If Mama would lend me her pretty pink shawl with the sequins, I could dance while Ella played the piano."

"Oh, you're always doing that," Charlotte said. "Why don't we all go down to Papa's shop? I bet there'll be a lot of peddlers there today 'cause it's raining."

The neighborhood peddlers were the children's friends. It would be great fun to see them, the five little girls agreed.

A small group of peddlers had already gathered around Papa's coal stove. There was Polack who had the heavy body and broad, stolid face of a Polish peasant. He was slumped down in one of Papa's chairs, his thick hands jammed into the pockets of his worn, patched trousers. One would think those trousers would stay up on his broad hips without the support of a belt but evidently Polack did not think so. About his middle he had wound a stout piece of rope and knotted it so tightly that the trousers looked as pleated as an accordion. The buttons on his ragged jacket had disappeared long ago so he used large safety pins in their place.

Close by sat Joe, a swarthy Italian. His working clothes, heavy blue denim overalls pulled over a blue denim shirt, were patched and faded, but neat. Joe always talked in lively fashion, waving his hands expressively. "Mucha rain! Bah! No gooda for business!" He repeated these words over and over in disgust. In a neglected heap on the floor beside him lay the sack in which he collected the junk he sold to Papa.

Picklenose was very sympathetic. For an hour this morning, he too had gone about as usual from yard to yard, calling loudly, "Any old rags and bottles to sell, any old clothes." But the housewives had paid no attention. He got nothing but wet clothes and wet feet for all his pains.

Poor old Picklenose! His face would have been most ordinary had he not been blessed with such an enormous object in the middle of it. It was a bulbous, fleshy nose, and not only did it glow red, but on its top grew a pickle-shaped wart which had given him his name.

"Pop," he called out, "got a piece of cardboard?"

"Look in the paper room," Papa told him.

Picklenose rose from his chair and made for the paper section. He returned soon with several pieces and sat down

again. Removing his wet shoes, he stared ruefully at his socks. They were soaked with water which had come through the torn soles. He removed the socks, rolled them into a ball, and stuffed them into his pocket. Then with a small jackknife he carefully cut the cardboard into the shape of soles which he placed inside the shoes.

"These will have to do until I get me some more money," he said, putting his shoes on again. He hunted in his pockets until he found his plug of tobacco. Politely offering some to the others, he also bit off a generous mouthful for himself. And so he sat, chewing and talking away at the same time.

Charlie was there, too. His tall, lanky body was settled comfortably in a tipped-back chair, his big feet resting on the little stove as he swung back and forth on the chair's back legs.

Charlie was different from the others. He was handsome, blond, and blue-eyed, and a good deal younger than most of the peddlers. It was rumored he had come from a wealthy family and had a fine education. But something had happened in Charlie's life that changed everything. No one really knew what, not even Papa who was Charlie's best friend. There were plenty of rumors, of course, but no one knew the real truth of any of them. Charlie himself never spoke about his past.

He was a good worker but worked only when he felt like it. Every so often he would disappear for days at a time. Nobody knew where to, nor why, nor when he would return. Back he always came though, a bit silent and unhappy looking, but ready to work again.

Papa was always glad when Charlie returned. It was not only because Charlie was Papa's right-hand man. There was something special between Papa and this tall fellow, a man-to-man something. Of course Papa loved his family, but sometimes he felt lonesome as the only man among six females. At such times there was always Charlie he could turn to for companionship.

The children adored Charlie too, especially Ella, who lately had begun to gaze at him with bright and shiny eyes and hang upon his every word. Charlie loved the children too and seemed at his happiest when doing something for them.

The children's entrance was hailed with pleasure. Their bright young faces brought sunshine into the gloomy cellar. Papa looked up to wave them a cheery hello, and returned to his bookkeeping, but Charlie set the front legs of his chair down with a bang. Jumping up, he picked up Gertie and tossed her high into the air. She squealed with delight and when he put her down, she cried, "Do it again, Charlie, again!" Charlie laughed and tossed her high once more.

Then he called out, "Hey, Papa, what about the surprise we have for the young ones?"

"Surprise! What kind of surprise? Tell us!" The children skipped back and forth between Charlie and Papa.

"Charlie," Papa said, "take them into the paper section and show them the load of books that came in this morning."

"Books!" The children all shouted at once. "Papa, how wonderful! How did you get them? You never got any books in before. Are there any children's books among them? May we have them?"

"Hey, one at a time! If you'll give me a chance to say something, I'll try to answer all those questions." The little girls quieted down and listened.

"A peddler brought them in. Some rich man uptown was moving and after going through his collection of books, he picked out this lot that he no longer wanted. He called in a peddler and sold them to him. And that's how I got them. I haven't had a chance to look them over, but if you want any, you'd better get in there and go through them. I expect to resell the whole lot this afternoon."

The children needed no urging. They rushed pell-mell into the paper section with Charlie at their heels. There on the floor in a tumbled mass lay the precious books. Charlie stood by and watched as they began to hunt eagerly through the piles.

Gertie did not yet know how to read. When she found there were no picture books, she picked up a magazine instead. She made her small self comfortable on a heap of old newspapers and turned the pages slowly. Book hunting was over for her.

Lucky Charlotte discovered a book of fairy tales almost immediately. A brand new book it was, still in its bright paper cover. It was written in simple language and printed in large black letters. She stood up, hugging the book to her and began at once to read. In no time at all, she was completely lost to the world about her. For her book hunting was over too.

As for Henny, she didn't even bother to hunt. She was having much more fun tossing the books back and forth to Charlie as if they were baseballs. "Hey," Ella called out, "aren't you going to help us look through these?"

"What for? You're good pickers. I'll be satisfied with whatever you pick out for me."

Ella and Sarah were the only systematic ones. They picked the books up one by one and looked through them carefully.

"Found anything yet?" Charlie asked.

"No," answered Sarah, "not yet. Most of these books look like studying books, not reading books."

"Look over here," Ella suddenly cried. "There are some reading books. See, there's a whole set of Dickens. There are

even some here that I've never heard of before. 'Sketches by Boz.' 'More Sketches by Boz.' " She looked up at Charlie with a shining face. "Oh, Charlie, do you think Papa will let us keep the whole set?"

"I don't know," replied Charlie, pleased with her good choice and her delight in it. "Better ask him yourself."

"Oh, but Ella," Sarah wailed, "they look like grown-up books. I won't be able to read them."

"Well," her sister replied, "if you can't read them now, you'll be able to when you're as old as I am."

"But that's so far off. I want something for now."

"Let's keep looking. Maybe we'll find something else."

They kept on looking and just when they were about ready to give up, they found the most wonderful "something for now" book imaginable. Ella and Sarah pounced on it and as soon as they turned the first page, they called out in excitement, "Charlotte, Gertie, Henny! Come quick! Just look at what we've found!"

Everybody gathered around. It was wonderful! Enchanting! It seemed like a bit of Fairyland come to life. They might have dreamed about such a book but they had not known that one like it even existed.

"Why, it's more than just a reading book!" Ella cried.

The book was called *The Dolls That You Love,* and on one side of each page was printed the story about the day's happenings, while on the other side were cutouts of the dolls and the clothes they wore.

"Aren't they sweet?" cried Charlotte, pointing to an adorable blue dress and bonnet that matched.

"See how many dresses they have to change into!" exclaimed Sarah. "Oh, how I wish we could start dressing them right now!"

"Why you could spend hours with them!"

"Ooh, look at this page! They show winter clothes and see, the story is about their going sleighing."

"Just the thing for a rainy day, isn't it?" Charlie said, happy in their happiness.

With the volumes of Dickens, the book of fairy tales, and *The Dolls That You Love* parceled out among them, they trooped back to the front of the shop to show Papa their finds.

"May we keep them all?" Ella asked.

When he said "Yes," they could hardly believe their ears. They never thought to own even one book and now they had twelve. It was too wonderful!

"Keep them for good? We don't have to give them back?" they asked again, just to hear Papa say, "Yes, they're yours," once more.

"All right now," Papa added. "Run along home and let me get some work done."

The children scurried up the basement stairs.

"I've got a wonderful idea," Sarah exclaimed. "You know what! Let's play library when we get home! I'll be the library lady and you must all come and get your books stamped by me."

Henny said, "Why should you be the library lady? I want to be the library lady."

"Me, too," added Charlotte.

"But it was my idea first," replied Sarah.

"Yes," agreed Ella, "it was Sarah's idea, and besides she'd make a good library lady." She laughed. "It'll be fun dressing you up. I'll comb your hair with a pompadour like hers."

"I can ask Mama to let me wear her old black skirt," Sarah said, "and when I walk, it'll swish and swirl all around the floor just like Miss Allen's."

"And I must come and ask you if you have a good book for me and you must smile and say, 'Yes, of course.'" Charlotte was already busy with her make believe.

"And I'll be noisy and you'll have to tell me, 'Shush!'"
Henny's eyes lit up.

"And can I look at the dolly book?" asked Gertie.

"Yes, you can look at it," Ella told her, "but you mustn't start dressing the dolls. We want to do that all together to-night."

"You know," Sarah said, "I never thought a rainy day could be such fun."

Who Cares If It's Bedtime?

MAMA'S YOUNGEST BROTHER Hyman had neither wife nor children of his own, so he came frequently to Mama's house to share in the life of the family.

Winter or summer, his favorite place would be before the kitchen stove. With his hands locked behind his back, and toes turned out, he would sway his short, stocky body from side to side. His jolly red face was shaped like the moon and shone just as brightly. Once Gertie had asked him "if he scrubbed it awful hard to make it so shiny." He had roared with good-natured laughter and then assured her that he never washed his face at all, that he had just been born that way.

Tonight, as usual, Uncle Hyman stayed for supper. He

ate his favorite meal of six hard-boiled eggs and half a loaf of sour rye bread spread thickly with butter.

Supper over, Hyman loosened his belt and gave his stomach several contented pats. Knowing that money was not too plentiful in the household, he not only insisted upon paying for his meal but distributed pennies to the delighted children as well.

"Now I'll have an extra penny to give the library lady on Friday," said Sarah.

The next day Gertie and Charlotte went to Mrs. Blumberg's candy store to spend Uncle Hyman's pennies.

"You still have the pennies, Charlotte?"

"Oh, you silly! You've asked me about a million times. Of course I have them!" Charlotte uncurled the fingers of her right hand and showed Gertie two pennies lying warm and moist in her palm.

When they reached the candy store, the two little girls stood before the glass cases so full of chewy and sucking delights and could not make up their minds. It was most important that they get something exactly right for tonight's fun in bed. It was hard to choose when everything looked so tempting.

From where she sat on a high stool in a corner of her shop, Mrs. Blumberg looked at them over the top of her glasses.

Ach, she thought to herself, they'll take their time. Well, let them enjoy themselves. She bent her head once again to the paper she was reading.

Gertie pointed to the chocolate-covered peanut bars. "Oh, look — Indian bars!"

"No," Charlotte replied at once. "You get too little. We'd finish in no time."

"Licorice drops take a long time to eat. Look how big they are!"

"Maybe," Charlotte hesitated for a moment and then shook her head. "No, they won't do. The pieces will all be the same."

They looked at the red cherry hearts, the yellow and orange "chicken-corn" candy, and the different-colored jelly beans.

"Charlotte, half a penny jelly beans and half a penny chicken-corn! That would be a whole lot of candy!"

"But we like the black jelly beans best and we can't ask Mrs. Blumberg to pick out only black ones for us. You know we hate the white ones and we always seem to get mostly white ones whenever we buy them. No, let's not take jelly beans."

Gertie's suggestion had given Charlotte an idea. "Mrs. Blumberg," she called out, "could we buy a quarter of a cent's worth of candy?"

"Woe is me! Haven't I got trouble enough giving you half a penny dis and half a penny dat? No, darling, for less than half a penny, I can't sell."

Charlotte sighed as she turned back to the cases. It would have been so nice to have four different kinds of candy all for one penny. She and Gertie continued their examinations. One by one, they talked over each kind only to reject it. Lemon drops you could only suck. Caramels had to be chewed so hard and so long. Chocolate pennies melted too quickly in your mouth. The children considered and considered.

Suddenly Charlotte saw the little people made out of chewy chocolate colored candy. "Gertie," she cried happily, "why didn't we notice them before? Chocolate babies!"

"Goody!" Gertie was equally pleased.

Now that this troublesome problem was solved, they were ready to get on with the spending of the second penny. With the bag of precious chocolate babies held tightly in Charlotte's hand, they walked to Mr. Basch's grocery store. Mr. Basch's store was right under Mama's front room. When the children practiced on their piano, the sounds came through the ceiling. At such times Mr. Basch often wished they would take themselves and their piano somewhere else. But he liked the children well enough when they were not practicing and came forward to greet them smilingly. He wore a little black skull cap on top of his white hair and all the time he talked, he smoothed and smoothed his silky white beard.

"Hello," he said in Yiddish. Mr. Basch spoke no English. "What does Mama want today?"

"Oh, we've come to buy something for ourselves," Charlotte told him, and she held up her penny.

"And what are you going to buy for that penny?"

"We thought we'd like some crackers — the broken kind."

The open cracker barrel held a most amazing jumble of broken crackers. No need to worry here about making a choice. A scoop from the barrel and into a paper bag went a tantalizing

assortment. The children turned over their penny to Mr. Basch and prepared to depart with their bagful.

"Wait a minute, children," Mr. Basch called. He walked over to the back of the store where he kept slabs of smoked salmon (he called it lox) and cut off two pieces of moist, salty skin. This was a rare treat.

The children sat down on the stoop in front of their house and sucked away at the bits of smoked salmon which still clung to the skin. Afterward they would be very thirsty, but right now they were enjoying themselves greatly.

"Good, isn't it?" Gertie said between noisy sucks.

When they had chewed up every scrap of fat and fish, they threw the skins away and remembered once more their bags of goodies. Charlotte tumbled the whole lot into her lap and both children looked at the pile with deep satisfaction.

"My, it's such a lot!" Gertie breathed. "Oh, couldn't we have a taste now, just a little, teeny taste?"

Charlotte was equally tempted. So they shared a broken cracker between them. And then it only seemed right that they should taste the chocolate babies too. They ate one of them. One taste led to another and pretty soon a second piece of cracker plus a second chocolate baby had disappeared.

"We'd better put everything away, or we'll be eating it all up," Charlotte decided. Everything went back into the bags.

"Will Mama let us take the bags to bed, Charlotte?"

"Of course not! I'm going to hide them."

"Where?"

"Under the pillows on our bed. Nobody would ever think of looking there."

They trotted upstairs. Mama was busy over the kitchen stove so she never noticed Charlotte slipping into the bedroom. The goodies were tied into one of Papa's large red handkerchiefs (paper bags rattled so) and the handkerchief was tucked under the large feather pillows on their bed. Now they had only to wait until bedtime.

Bedtime came early for Mama's girls. The children were sent to bed at the same time regardless of age. Mama had found that to be much the best way for all. In the first place, the children had no feeling of separation from each other as they would have had if they went to bed at different times. And it meant that Mama could have a few quiet hours for reading or knitting or even just chatting with Papa without being disturbed by her little ones.

As for the children, bedtime was something to which they

looked forward. Bedtime was when Ella and Sarah, who slept together, built their imaginary house and decorated the beautifully rich and colorful make-believe rooms. Bedtime was when Charlotte made up fanciful stories to tell or thought up games to play with her bedfellow, Gertie. Bedtime was when Henny planned some special mischief she could carry on the next day in school or at home. Planned all by herself, because she did not like sharing a bed with anyone.

They slept, all five of them, in the one room and that made for plenty of company in the dark. And what was the best of all, Mama never minded their talking to each other. "It's early enough and they're resting their bodies anyway," she said. "They'll fall asleep when they get tired."

"Come on. Let's get under the covers quickly. It's freezing in here tonight," Charlotte said as she and Gertie ran towards their bed.

"Where's the candy?" Gertie asked, when they were settled.

"Here," Charlotte said. "Before Mama came in here to fold up the bedspreads, I sneaked in and put the stuff on the floor." She leaned over her side of the bed, poked about for a bit and came up with the red handkerchief bundle.

She laid the bundle between them. Mama was coming in now with the heated flatirons. They slapped their hands over the handkerchief and lay still, quivering with mischief and excitement. It would be awful if Mama were to remove that heap of goodies. Gertie started to giggle but a nudge from Charlotte soon stopped her. Mama went about putting the irons first into Ella's and Sarah's bed, next in Henny's and now she was coming over to them.

The room was in darkness save for the gas light which shone from the kitchen through the opened bedroom door. Lucky for them! One look at their guilty faces, and Mama would have known that something was up. But Mama suspected nothing. She put the iron wrapped in its towel at their feet and their toes stretched out deliciously to meet the warmth. Tucking in the featherbed, Mama said good night to all and went out, shutting the bedroom door behind her.

The fun could begin at last! Charlotte directed because the game was hers.

"First we take a chocolate baby, and we eat only the head." They bit off the heads and chewed away contentedly.

"Now the feet." That was hard. The tiny feet were very close to the legs but they did the best they could.

"Let's gobble the rest up altogether." That was a good order. They gobbled away.

Charlotte continued. "A cracker now." They fished about in the dark. "We'll take a small bite just to find out what kind it is."

They each took a small bite. "Mine is a lemon snap, I think," Gertie said. "What's yours?"

"Mine's a ginger. We have to nibble along the side of this piece of cracker as if we were mice and we have to do it until I say stop." So they nibbled and nibbled and pretty soon Gertie exclaimed, "My piece is all gone."

"So's mine," Charlotte told her. She had enjoyed nibbling so much she had forgotten to change the order.

"That means we'll have to take another cracker." So they took another cracker. The tasting bite showed to their delight that they had each chosen the same kind, chocolate snaps.

"First we're to count up to ten before we begin eating." They counted slowly. "Now," continued Charlotte, "we must each take a teensy, weensy bite and chew five times." That was done. "The rest of the cracker has to be chewed for twenty-five counts." They bit and chewed while Charlotte counted very fast because crackers become nothing in your mouth quickly and it would never do if the eating was over before the counting. Gertie felt anxious. Her piece of cracker was small, but luckily, it came out all right.

Charlotte had lots of ideas. With the next cracker they had to make a circling movement ten times around in front of their open mouths and then pop the cracker in. But they were not to bite into it. Oh no, that cracker had to be taken out of their mouths again and the circle repeated ten times. After that they could eat the cracker as they pleased.

And so the game was played till there wasn't a single thing left. They had not been interrupted even once throughout the whole time because their sisters were busy too. Ella and Sarah were decorating the Pink Room in the make-believe house. They had been having a good deal of trouble deciding about the placing of the furniture.

Henny was fretting over a new trouble. She had not done her homework for several days. Teacher had given her a note that Mama was to sign because teacher wanted to make sure that Mama knew about this. Henny was trying to figure out some way of getting Mama to sign the note without having to take a spanking too.

Suddenly Gertie said, "I'm thirsty."

"Me, too," said Charlotte. She sat up in bed and called, "Ma, may we have some water?"

Mama brought the water, wondering at the unusual request. She found the reason why the next morning when she made up the cracker-crumbed bed.

There was no game for Charlotte and Gertie the next night. "We'll just have to stick to candy from now on," Charlotte decided.

Stick to candy they did. Often and often the game was played and Mama never knew — or so at least they thought.

The Sabbath

THE SABBATH BEGINS Friday evening at dusk and for two days Mama was busy with her preparations. On Fridays she cleaned, cooked, and baked. On Thursdays she shopped. Sabbath meals had to be the best of the whole week so it was most important that she shop carefully. Every Thursday afternoon, Mama went to Rivington Street market where prices were lower than in her neighborhood stores.

Usually she left Gertie in Papa's care and set off alone right after lunch. This Thursday Mama was rather late. The children would soon be home from school so Mama decided that it would be nice if for once shopping for the Sabbath could be a family affair.

"Who wants to come to market with me?" she asked the children as soon as they came trooping in.

"I do! I do!" Everybody wanted to go along.

"Gracious, hasn't anybody any other plans for this afternoon?" asked Mama.

"Nothing as exciting as going to market," Ella declared, and her sisters all agreed.

But what about Gertie? It was a long walk for little feet.

Gertie spoke up as if she knew what Mama was thinking. "Oh, Mama," she pleaded, "me too!"

Mama wasn't going to disappoint her. "All right, but I think it would be a good idea to take the baby carriage along."

"Baby carriage!" Gertie was indignant. "I'm too big for a baby carriage!"

"Of course you are," Mama assured her, "but the carriage will come in handy for all the bundles and if you should happen to get too tired to keep on walking, why, we can have the bundles move over and make room for a very nice little girl. Now hurry, everybody. Into your hats and coats."

"Mama," said Sarah, "we'll be passing right by the library. Couldn't we go up for just a minute so you could meet the library lady?"

"Well — I don't know. I have a lot of shopping to do." Mama hesitated. "I would like to see her."

"Please, Mama, for just a minute."

"She's asked us a number of times to bring you over," Ella said.

"All right," replied Mama. "But we can't stay long."

The children were pleased. At last the library lady was going to see Mama. The children were very proud of Mama. Most of the other Jewish women in the neighborhood had such bumpy shapes. Their bodies looked like mattresses tied about in the middle. But not Mama. She was tall and slim and held herself proudly. Her face was proud too.

Once inside the library, the children scrambled eagerly up the stairs while Mama followed at a more sedate pace. They stood in a small group waiting for a moment when the library lady would be free. Then Sarah approached the desk.

Miss Allen looked up and smiled. "Hello, Sarah. It can't be Friday already?"

"No," laughed Sarah. "It's only Thursday, but we brought Mama."

"How nice!" the library lady said, and came from behind her desk to join the family.

"Mama," said Sarah proudly, "this is Miss Allen."

"I'm so glad you came," said the library lady as she extended her hand in greeting. "My, you couldn't possibly be the mother of five — you look young enough to be their eldest sister."

"I don't feel that young," said Mama laughing. "But thank you for the compliment. I've been wanting to meet you for a long time. But you know how it is with a family this size. There's always something to do. The children talk about you so much at home though, I feel that I already know you."

"They've told me all about you, too," replied Miss Allen.

"Sarah has never forgotten your kindness to her," continued Mama. "For that matter, all the children are always telling me such nice things about you. How you're always ready with a suggestion about what they should read, and how interested you are in discussing the books with them. I appreciate that."

"It's a pleasure to help such eager readers," the librarian said, smiling at the upturned faces.

"Well," Mama said, beaming, "I'm afraid we'll have to be running along."

"We're all going to market," Sarah explained.

"Good," said Miss Allen, "and when you come tomorrow, you can tell me all about it."

"Do you like her, Mama?" asked Sarah as they walked downstairs.

"Yes," answered Mama. "She's very sweet — and so pretty too!" Mama was thoughtful for a moment. She turned to Ella and added, "She smiles at you, but somehow the face is wistful, don't you think?"

Back on the street, the children danced along sometimes beside, sometimes just behind Mama. That is, all except Henny. She kept racing ahead and dashing back again, just like a small, impatient puppy.

Already their ears were filled with the shrill cries of street hawkers. Already they could smell the good smells, and in another minute, they were themselves part of the crowd.

"Just look at all the pushcarts!" exclaimed Sarah.

Heaped high with merchandise, they stretched in endless lines up and down the main street and in and out the side streets. They were edged up close to the curb and wedged together so tightly that one could not cross anywhere except at the corners. The pushcart peddlers, usually bearded men in long overcoats or old women in heavy sweaters and shawls, out-

67

did each other in their loud cries to the passers-by. All promised
bargains — bargains in everything — in fruits and vegetables,
crockery, shoelaces, buttons, and other notions, in aprons and
housedresses, in soap and soap powders, and hundreds of other
things.

There were stores in which you could buy fish and stores that carried only dairy products. There were bakeries and meat shops, shoe stores and clothing establishments. In delicatessen shops, fat "specials" (frankfurters) hung on hooks driven into the walls and big chunks of "knubble" (garlic) wurst were laid

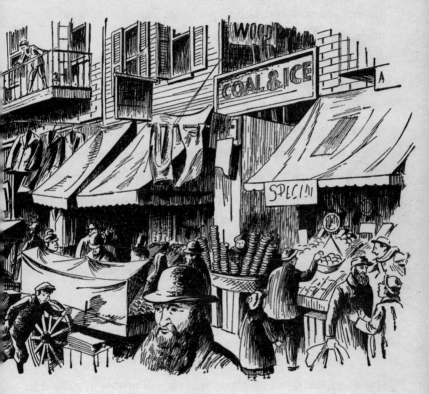

out in neat rows on white trays which bore the sign "A Nickel a Schtickel" (a nickel for a piece). The counters overflowed with heaps of smoked whitefish and carp, and large slabs of smoked red salmon. If one wished, firm plump salt herrings were fished out of barrels for inspection before buying. Men's red flannel drawers and ladies' petticoats flew in the wind from their show-hooks on dry-goods store fronts.

But it was not enough that the merchandise sold behind closed shop doors could be displayed in showcase windows and store fronts. Their owners had to come out in the open too. They built stands which they either used themselves or rented out to others. Almost anything could be bought at these stands. There were pickle stands where the delicious odor of sour pickles mingled with the smell of sauerkraut and pickled tomatoes and watermelon rind. There were stands where only cereal products were sold — oats, peas, beans, rice and barley — all from open sacks. At other stands, sugar and salt were scooped out of large barrels and weighed to order. Here coffee was bought in the bean, for every household had its own wooden coffee grinder.

And wherever there was a bit of space too small for a regular stand, one could be sure to find the old pretzel woman. Her wrinkled face was almost hidden inside of the woolen kerchief bound round her head. Her old hands trembled as they wrapped up the thick, chewy pretzels.

The sidewalks were choked with people. It was not easy for Mama to push the carriage through the narrow aisles left between pushcarts and stands. The children followed behind in twos and whenever Mama stopped either to buy or look, they stopped too.

"Say, Gertie," Charlotte cried out, "how would you like a necklace like that?" She pointed to the garlic peddler who was coming towards them. No need for a store, a stand, or a pushcart for this peddler. With a basket full of garlic on one arm and a spicy necklace of the same looped around his neck, he was all set for business.

The dried mushroom peddlers did business in the same way except that, as Charlotte laughingly said, "They were better dressed." They wore long, heavy mushroom bracelets about their arms as well as necklaces.

How sharply the shoppers hunted for bargains! And what bargains, if one could believe the peddlers. How carefully every article was examined to make sure it was perfect! It always was, according to the shopkeepers. How the buyers haggled over the price of everything. And how the peddlers swore on their very lives that the price of anything was the lowest at which they could afford to part with it! But above and through all the noise and confusion, ran a feeling of great good nature and cheery contentment.

Only one tongue was spoken here — Yiddish. It was like a foreign land right in the midst of America. In this foreign land, it was Mama's children who were the foreigners since they alone conversed in an alien tongue — English.

At the next corner, Henny bought a fat, juicy sour pickle with her after-lunch penny. She ate it greedily, with noise and gusto, while her sisters watched, their mouths watering. "Selfish! How about giving us a taste, huh?"

Henny pretended that she didn't hear them, but before the pickle was half gone, she stopped teasing and gave each a bite.

Inside Mama's favorite fish store the smell was not so pleasing. "Gertie," suggested Charlotte, "let's squeeze our noses tight and talk to each other while we're squeezing."

And that's just what they did, talking about anything at all just so they could hear the funny sounds which came through their squeezed noses. "Look at the big fish with goggly eyes," said Gertie.

"I hope Mama is not getting any live fish this week," Charlotte said. "I like to see them swimming around in the bathtub but I don't like it when Papa cleans them afterward."

But Mama was not getting any live fish this time, only pieces of several different kinds of fish, whitefish, yellow pike and winter carp — that meant gefüllte fish (stuffed fish) for the Sabbath, yum, yum!

"I wish Mama would hurry up," said Gertie. "I can smell the fish right through my squeezed nose. And I do want to buy something for my penny, don't you?"

"Yes, and no fish!"

Out on the street again, the air seemed sharper and colder. Some of the peddlers had been standing in their places since early morning. They stamped their feet and slapped their arms across their chests trying to warm their chilled bones. But the sweet potato man did not mind the cold. Why should he when he had his nice hot street oven to push before him? When Ella caught sight of him, she said at once, "Just the thing for a cold day." The sweet potato man stopped before her and pulled open one of the drawers of his oven. There arose on the air such a delicious smell that Ella smacked her lips expectantly. Inside she saw the plump sweet potatoes in their gray jackets.

Some were cut open in halves and their rich golden color gave promise of great sweetness. For her penny, Ella got a large half and as she bit into it, she wondered why sweet potatoes baked at home never tasted half so good. When she rejoined the family, four other mouths helped to make short work of that potato.

The chicken market was the next stopping place. It was smelly and noisy with the squawking of fowl. The children gathered about the crates and watched the roosters sticking their long necks through the slats. Mama donned an apron she had

brought with her and began to pluck the fowl she selected.

After Mama finished her plucking, the chicken was wrapped up and added to the other bundles in the shopping bag. The family continued on its way.

Gertie turned to Charlotte. "What'll we buy with our pennies?" The answer to that question was just then coming along the street. Candied slices of tangerine and candied grapes mounted on sticks lay in rows on white trays. The peddler stopped when he heard Gertie's delighted cry. "Penny a stick, little darlings," he said. Charlotte chose grape and Gertie took tangerine. Thus two more pennies were spent.

"I'm almost through," Mama told them, but still Sarah's penny lay warm and snug in her coat pocket. "Aren't you going to spend your penny?" the children asked her. They couldn't be sure because Sarah was saving all her pennies these days — six for the dolly and one penny for the library lady. But today was something special. She had shared in the goodies her sisters had bought. It would only be fair for her to return their generosity. But what could she get?

"Arbis! Shaynicke, guttinke arbislach! Keuf meine heise arbis!" (Chick peas. Fine, nice chick peas. Buy my hot chick peas!)

The hot-chick-pea peddler was singing the words over and over in a funny Yiddish chant as he rolled a small white oven along the streets. Before Mama could stop her, mischievous Henny gave the carriage a big push so that it rolled away from under Mama's hands. She stooped over it as if she were pushing a great weight and began to chant in imitation:

"*Arbis! Shaynicke, guttinke arbislach!*"

The children roared with laughter. Even Mama could not hide a smile while she ordered Henny to stop. "Leave her alone, lady," the peddler told Mama. "She's helping me in mine business."

Because he was so good-natured, Sarah decided to give up her penny to him. Everyone watched as he fished out the peas. First he took a small square of white paper from a little compartment on one side of the oven. He twirled the paper about his fingers to form the shape of a cone and then skillfully twisted the pointed end so that the container would not fall apart. He lifted the wagon cover on one side revealing a large white enamel pot. The steam from the pot blew its hot breath in the little girls' faces so they stepped back a bit while the peas were ladled out with a big soup spoon. The wagon cover was dropped back into place and the paper cup handed over to

Sarah. The peas were spicy with pepper and salt, and how good they were! They warmed up the children's tummies and made them very thirsty.

With the purchase of a pound of pumpernickel bread, the shopping tour came to an end. They left behind the life and activity of the market and started the weary walk home. By now the children were tired. Gertie uttered not a single word of protest when Mama lifted her up and put her into the carriage together with the bundles. The others wished they were young enough to join her.

The next afternoon, when they had chosen their books, they told the library lady all about their marketing trip. Ella was a good actress and could imitate voice and gestures marvelously well. The children and the library lady went into gales of laughter as she mimicked the various peddlers. They made so much noise that the other librarian stared at them reprovingly.

"I guess we'd better be quiet," Miss Allen whispered.

The children started for the staircase walking exaggeratedly on tiptoes and giggling softly.

At home, the kitchen was warm with the smell of fresh-baked white bread. The room sparkled with cleanliness. The table, which wore only an oilcloth covering all through the week, now had on a snowy white tablecloth. On it stood the brass candlesticks, gleaming brightly from the polishing that Ella and Sarah had given them the day before. They were just in time to see Mama saying the prayer over the candles.

The children stood around the table watching her. A lovely feeling of peace and contentment seemed to flow out from Mama to them. First she put a napkin on her head; then placing four white candles in the brass candlesticks, she lit them. She extended her arms to form a circle. Over the lighted candles the encircling gesture was repeated. After that Mama covered her eyes with her hands, softly murmuring a prayer in Hebrew.

Thus was the Sabbath ushered in.

Mama set two braided loaves of white bread on the table at Papa's place. She covered them with a clean white napkin. Then from the whatnot, she took a wine bottle full of the dark sweet red wine which Papa always made himself. She also took a small wine glass and put these on the table next to the loaves.

The children lined up before Papa. He placed his hand on each child's head, asking God's blessing for his little one. When this ceremony was over, Papa left for the synagogue.

It's so lovely and peaceful, thought Ella. Now if only Charlie were here, everything would be just perfect. Had Mama invited him for the Sabbath supper? She hadn't said.

"Is Charlie coming tonight?" she asked.

"No," answered Mama. "Papa tells me Charlie hasn't been in the shop for over a week."

So Charlie was gone again. For how long this time, wondered Ella.

"Where do you suppose he goes?"

"Who knows?" Mama answered with a sigh.

"Doesn't Papa ever ask him?"

Mama shook her head. "You don't ask people about their personal lives."

"It's queer. Charlie isn't at all like the other peddlers, is he, Mama? He seems so educated and so fine. Why does he live like this? What do you suppose happened to him?" Ella's questions caught the attention of the other children.

"I guess he likes it this way," Henny remarked airily.

"Has he a Mama and a Papa?" Sarah asked. She could not imagine life without parents.

"We don't know, Sarah. He never mentions them."

"He comes and goes," began Charlotte.

Henny finished, "And nobody knows."

Papa came in. "Good Sabbath," he said.

"Good Sabbath," each replied.

Papa washed his hands. It was time for supper, but first he must pronounce the prayer in praise of his wife for her fine Sabbath preparations. Then he must say a prayer of thanksgiving for the Sabbath. To do this, Papa filled the glass full of wine, raised it aloft and said a short prayer in Hebrew, then drank some of it. Everyone had a sip from the glass.

Another short prayer was said over the loaves. Papa uncovered them and cut a thick piece for Mama and smaller pieces for the girls. In turn, Mama and the children recited the prayer thanking God for giving them this bread. Now, at last, supper could be eaten.

Such a good supper! *Gefüllte* fish, chicken soup with homemade noodles, chicken, carrots prepared in a sweet way, and applesauce.

Afterward, the children helped with the clearing of the table and the dishwashing. In the lovely hush of the Sabbath eve, they once more gathered around the table, the children with their books, Mama with her magazine, and Papa with his Jewish newspaper. All heads were bent low over their reading while the candles flickered and sputtered. It was quiet except for the whispered sounds of Charlotte's voice as she read aloud from her primer to wide-eyed Gertie.

So they would continue reading until the candles burnt low. Then they would undress and go to bed — for after the candles died out, the room would be in complete darkness. There could be no light struck on the Sabbath. That was the law.

Papa's Birthday

THE MONTH OF DECEMBER was almost over. In another week the fifth of January would be upon them. That day was Papa's birthday. The children had decided they were going to do something special about it. Ella had called a secret meeting to talk it over.

As soon as Mama had shut the bedroom door that night, Henny, Gertie, and Charlotte left the comfort of their own beds to join Ella and Sarah in theirs. With them went their pillows. Up against the wall which hemmed the bed on one side went five pillows. Up against the pillows went five wriggling, giggling little girls. Up to their necks went the coverlet.

"Stop humping your knees up there, Henny," complained

Charlotte, shivering. "You're letting all the cold air come in."

"Well, this cover was meant to be used up and down and not sideways. It's just not wide enough. If I put my knees down, my toes will stick out."

"Ella is taller than you," retorted Sarah, "but her toes don't stick out. Why is that?"

"I'm sitting up and Henny is lying down, that's why," Ella explained. "Henny, you stop trying to be so comfortable and sit up like the rest of us."

Henny sat up and the meeting could begin. Ella spoke first. "I think we're old enough to buy a present for Papa this year."

"Yes — but where would we get the money?" Sarah was always the practical one.

"If we all saved our pennies for the next week, we'd have enough money," Ella said.

"I'll save my pennies," Gertie chimed in.

"But that won't leave us any money to spend for a whole week," wailed Henny. "We won't be able to buy any candy or anything for a *whole week?*"

"Well, can't you give up your candy for a week?" Ella demanded.

Henny wasn't so sure, but the others were. The present had to be from all of them equally.

"What about the library lady?" Sarah reminded them. "We promised to give her a penny every Friday."

"Oh, dear," said Ella. "I forgot all about that."

"Aren't we finished paying for that old book yet?" asked Henny.

"The library lady said we'll be all paid up in about three weeks," Sarah said.

"That's just fine!" Henny retorted. "Only Papa's birthday is next week."

"Maybe she'll let us skip a week," suggested Charlotte.

Sarah wouldn't hear of it. "But we promised. I don't want to skip a week." She thought for a moment. After all, she was the one who lost the book. It was up to her to figure out something. "Listen," she said firmly, "I've been saving all this time and I have a lot of money in my penny bank now. When Friday comes, I'll just take out five cents and bring them to the library lady."

So it was decided.

"Now the next thing is, it's got to be a surprise," Ella continued. "You mustn't even tell Mama about it."

The children all promised to keep the secret. They also promised to turn over their pennies to Ella each day as soon as they got them.

"But what are we going to buy for all that money?" Sarah asked.

"We'll worry about that when we have the money," Ella said. "We'll all go to the store together to choose something."

The following week was a very long one for the children. The pennies Mama handed out after lunch were faithfully turned over to Ella. She put them in a white pillbox which was full to busting by the end of the week. Thirty-five cents seemed like a small fortune; the children were sure they could get something very special for all that money.

The fifth was on a Sunday. Among Jewish people the Sabbath is on Saturday so stores are open on Sunday. Mama thought the children were out playing that afternoon, but they had gone instead to Mr. Pincus's bargain store. Mr. Pincus was a short man with what Gertie called "a stomach what sticks out." He had not a single hair on his head but he grew plenty of hair on his face to make up for that lack. He tried hard to be helpful.

"How about a nize ledder pocketbook dat he can carry

his money in?" he suggested. "Id only custs dirty-nine cents."

"But we only have thirty-five cents," Ella told him.

"Led me see. Here's a knife which he can carry aroun' in his pocked. Very handy. And id custs unly dirty-tree cents. Wid de change, you could buy yourselves someding."

"Yes, yes, let's take that," Henny cried. They could buy a lot of candy for two cents.

"But Papa already has a knife," Sarah reminded her.

Mr. Pincus began to walk up and down the store slowly.

The children trailed behind and carefully scanned every shelf. Whenever an item was suggested by one of the little company, the others either found it unsuitable or the price was wrong. They couldn't buy fancy garters to hold up the long sleeves of Papa's shirts because they could not agree on the colors. Sarah suggested a tie but that cost only twenty-five cents. What would they do with the remaining ten? It was too much for themselves and too little with which to buy something else. Charlotte thought a shirt would be a wonderful gift, but the cost was way beyond what they could afford.

Mr. Pincus began to mop his bald head with his handkerchief. It was warm work for a fat man, this pulling things off high shelves and putting them back again. The girls were beginning to feel unhappy.

"We should have asked Charlie," Ella said. "He would know what Papa likes."

Suddenly Gertie spied something. "Look at the pretty cup and saucer."

Her sisters looked and there arose a chorus of oh's and ah's. It was the most wonderful cup and saucer they had ever seen. They were all agreed on that. It was made of lustrous pink and white china and on its front, raised gold lettering marched proudly uphill to spell out the name "FATHER."

Mr. Pincus beamed. "She's a good picker, dat liddle one. Vait, I vanna show you someding."

He took the cup and saucer off the shelf and pointed with a stubby finger to a narrow ledge placed across one side of the cup. "You see dis? Dis is for de moustache. Id shouldn't ged ved. And your Papa he has a moustache. Id acshually custs dirty-seven cents but I'm gonna gif id to you for dirty-five cents so you should be able to gif your Papa a fine present."

Ella counted out the pennies and Mr. Pincus wrapped up the present for them. The sale over, the children took turns carrying the package home.

That night, they waited impatiently for Papa's homecoming. The present, in its neat wrapper, lay at his place on the table. Gertie and Charlotte hopped about excitedly, saying over and over, "I wish Papa would come! Oh, I wish Papa would come!"

Papa came at last. His steps on the stairs were slow and heavy tonight. It had been a long hard day at the shop with very little business done. Papa looked very tired.

But the children were too eager to spring their surprise to notice. They crowded about him, crying, "Happy birthday,

Papa! Happy birthday to you!" They could barely wait.

He smiled a weary little smile. "Thank you all for remembering," he said and started to wash up for supper. Mama, meanwhile, busied herself with putting the hot food on the table.

"Supper is ready," she called.

There was a rush. The children took their usual places quickly. They did not want to miss seeing Papa's face when he found the present.

"What's this?" he asked as he sat down.

"A present from your daughters," Mama told him.

"A present for me?" He'd never gotten a present from the children before. He couldn't quite believe it. Picking up the package he turned it round and round in his hands.

"Aren't you going to open it?" Henny asked.

"Yes, of course." Papa tugged at the cord, the wrapper fell away and the cup and saucer stood in splendor on the table. Papa stared at his present and said not a word.

The children were bewildered. What was wrong? What made Papa's face look so sorrowful? Didn't he like their present?

Papa was thinking: So much money spent on a fancy cup and saucer that I could just as well do without. Haven't we enough cups and saucers in the house now? I have to work so hard to make enough for the necessary things and here they spend money on such a luxury. What if the amount they spent wouldn't help much. It's little spendings like this that add up.

But right through his thoughts, there floated a little disappointed whimper from Gertie, and Papa suddenly remembered his children. He looked down at their faces, so puzzled and sad now. They had been so gay a moment ago. They were young. It was bad enough that they had to be denied so many things because he couldn't afford them. Must he deny them even this pleasure of giving up their small allowance for a present for him?

Ella interrupted his thoughts. She spoke quietly. "Perhaps we should have bought something more useful?"

Papa smiled his wide, gentle smile at his daughters. "No, no, it's wonderful! I've been wanting just such a cup and saucer for years. How did you ever come to think of it? I couldn't tell you right off how happy it made me because I was speechless with delight. Mama, pour me a cup of coffee right now. I can't wait to use my beautiful present."

Again the room flowed over with sunshine and happiness. Papa suddenly found himeslf covered over with five laughing daughters who tried to hug and kiss him all at the same time.

Purim Play

"Purim Day! Purim Day!" Charlotte and Gertie clapped their hands as they danced around the bedroom one morning late in March.

"Today is Purim!" Ella and Sarah sat up in bed and hugged each other.

"Hurray for Purim!" Henny threw off the covers, stood up in her bed, and bounced up and down excitedly.

Hundreds and hundreds of years ago, in the land of Persia, a wicked man named Haman had cast lots for a day on which to hang all the Jews. That was how the name of Purim first came into being for it means the Feast of Lots. Why all the gladness then? Because Haman had failed to accomplish this evil deed. He himself was hanged on the very gallows which he had caused to be built for the Jews. And ever since, this day of Purim has been celebrated with gaiety and laughter, feasting and singing, with masquerade and play.

The bedroom door flew open and there stood Mama. On her face was a smudge of flour and on her house dress the brown stain of prunes. "Henny," she said, "I don't think that bouncing is good for the bedsprings."

"Maybe not," replied Henny cheerfully, "but it's certainly good for me."

"Well, you just bounce yourself right out of that bed and into your clothes."

On Mama's face was a big smile. She liked Purim too. "Papa will be leaving for the synagogue right after breakfast," she announced. "If any of you want to go along, you'll have to hurry."

The children hurried with their dressing, through breakfast, and with the breakfast dishes. It was so cozy in the warm kitchen full of the smell of hot-from-the-oven Haman taschen. Haman taschen is the name given to triangular-shaped cakes filled to bursting with poppy seeds or prunes. Mama had baked two platters full and still kept making more. Henny tried to help herself to one of the delicious cakes, but Mama caught her in the act. "You can't have these now," she said. "They're too hot. You'll get your fill of them after lunch."

"Aren't you going to make any Teiglech?" Henny asked anxiously. Teiglech are fried balls of dough soaked in honey.

"They'll all be made by the time you get back from synagogue," Mama assured her.

Armed with rattle-wheels and horns, Papa and the children left the house. They were a merry group, with the five little girls dancing circles around Papa all the way. It was wonderful to be young today. Nobody cared how much noise they made. They pranced and shouted, tooted their horns and whirled their clappers, and grownups only smiled. Not a single cross word nor a grumble could be heard. Friends and relatives showered them with happy Purim greetings; even strangers hailed them as they passed on the streets.

As the family climbed the wooden staircase to the tiny place of worship, their noses were at once met by the familiar synagogue smell. It was a mingled smell of tabac, a snuff used freely by the older members of the congregation, old and yellowing prayer books, clothes, people.

The children loved coming here. Always they would gaze

with reverent awe at the red velvet curtains richly embroidered in gold, which hung before the place where the five books of the Torah were kept. The Torah are large parchment scrolls made of goatskin and sewed together with goat-gut. They tell in Hebrew writing done by hand the history, the laws, and religious customs of the Jewish people.

Twice a week a new portion of the Torah is begun. In Papa's synagogue the reading took place on an enclosed platform raised a few feet above the floor, like a small stage. The reading was not always done by the same member of the congregation, but no matter who was the chosen one, the pattern of reading remained the same. He would chant, sometimes loudly, sometimes softly in singsong manner, his body swaying forward and back or from side to front, in rhythm with his words. From two long rows of hard wooden benches, the men would join their leader in prayer and song. On the important holidays when women came too, they would sit at the back, separated from the menfolks by a drawn curtain. On such occasions, higher pitched intonings mingled with the male chantings, so that the room was filled with a constant hum of sound.

But today the hum swelled to excitement pitch. Papa stood the children up on the bench beside him. The tale of Purim was being read and though they could not understand the Hebrew words, they all knew the story well and their ears were ever ready to catch the name of Haman. Every time this name was mentioned, the din was terrific. The rattle-wheels were rattled, the horns were tooted, the children stamped with their feet. Those less fortunate ones who had brought no noisemakers used their hands and feet to add to the noise. When the whole story had been told and Haman had received his full share of noisy punishment from the congregation, services were over.

At home again, Mama had lunch and the Purim baskets ready. Lunch today held little interest for the children, except, of course, for the dessert of Haman taschen and Teiglech. But the Purim baskets were something else again. Their white napkin covers were lifted and the tempting contents of fruits, nuts, candy, and cake exclaimed over. These were to be delivered to friends and relatives and the girls were to be the messengers.

"Mama, which one is for the library lady?" asked Sarah. "You said you'd make one."

"I didn't make one yet," replied Mama. "Don't you remember that today is Sunday? The library is closed."

Sarah wailed disappointedly. "Why did Purim have to come on a Sunday this year?"

"It's not so bad, Sarah," Mama consoled her. "You can take it to her tomorrow, and we'll make the basket look especially nice. I have saved some of my finest Haman taschen just for her. When she takes a bite out of one of my Haman taschen, she'll say it's the best she ever tasted," Mama ended proudly.

Ella burst out laughing. "Mama! She's probably never tasted Haman taschen in her whole life. She wouldn't even know what they are."

Mama smiled. "Oh, I keep forgetting she's a gentile."

Sarah was not satisfied, however. "But I wanted her to see us all dressed up."

"Oh, my goodness!" Mama was horrified at the idea. "You couldn't go to the library in masquerade."

"Why not?" asked Henny. "Everybody knows it's Purim."

"Yes, but not in a library. In a library you're supposed to be quiet and not create a rumpus. You can tell her all about it tomorrow and I'm sure she'll find it very interesting. Come now — the baskets are waiting."

First, though, they had to get into their masquerade costumes. The hilarious business of dressing up began.

Ella had borrowed cousin Adolph's suit. Boys' clothes were strange things, she thought, as she stood looking down at the knickers she had slipped on. They flopped way down on her legs to meet the tops of her high-button shoes. Her sisters took one look and shrieked with laughter.

"Hey, why don't you hitch up your pants?" yelled Henny.

"I can't. They're too long. You know Adolph is taller than me."

Mama then helped her by pinning the cuffs of the knickers with safety pins so that they fitted close at the kneecap. The pants billowed out about her legs as if they were full of air. "Who cares?" said Ella. "We're supposed to look funny." She tucked the boy's shirt inside the pants and tied one of Papa's ties about her neck. Then on went Adolph's jacket and gone were Ella's arms. They were lost somewhere inside the too-long sleeves. As for the jacket's length and breadth, nothing could be done about that. Ella pinned up her long black hair tightly with some of Mama's hairpins and Adolph's roomy cap hid it all nicely. She paraded up and down the kitchen, the very picture of a ragamuffin.

In the meantime, Sarah was busy too. She was helped into one of Mama's old dresses and a worn-out jacket. Mama combed her hair so that it lay piled on her head in grown-up fashion; on top of that, a hat perched perilously. One toss of Sarah's head and the hat sailed across the kitchen floor. The sisters shrieked with laughter again. A hatpin was called into action and this time the hat was pinned into place. For final decoration, a veil was tied about the hat and crossed in a bow under the little girl's chin. Now if only she could walk without tripping over Mama's long skirt. She tested it out by taking very short steps but it was no use. The skirt twisted itself about her feet. Rip, rip, rip! It was pulled away from the waistband and Sarah's underwear peeked out through the torn place in the skirt.

"I can fix that in a minute," Mama assured her and out came the sewing box.

"You're fixing it now but what if it happens again when I walk through the streets?"

Charlotte had a good idea. "Why couldn't Mama sew a long piece of tape on the bottom of the skirt? She could make a loop on the other end and you could wear the loop around your arm. Then you could hold up your skirt just like the swell ladies in the picture magazines."

While Mama sewed, the other three children dressed. Four-year-old Gertie wearing the outfit of a sister of ten looked comical enough to wish for no other costume. And Charlotte was equally satisfied to masquerade as big sister Ella. As for Henny, she hunted in Mama's rag bag. With a few pieces of colored rags she turned out an amazing costume. An old red flannel petticoat, full of holes, was slipped over her own dress and pinned on. A piece of black rag became a shawl for her shoulders, hiding the pins as well. With one of Papa's large colored handkerchiefs tied about her small blonde head, she looked like a little old pretzel woman.

The messengers were now ready. Sarah strutted about, lifting her skirt high on one side. She approached Ella. "Sir," she said in a very grown-up manner, "would you please escort me to Tanta Rivka's house?"

Ella bowed in manly fashion. "Certainly, Madame, I should be most delighted to do so," and she offered Sarah her arm.

The Purim baskets were gathered up, and Mama issued instructions about their delivery. The little troupe sailed out of the house and into the streets so full now with other masqueraders carrying just such Purim baskets.

The first stop was on Sheriff Street where Tanta Rivka (Aunt Rebecca) lived in a small group of boxlike rooms, called a flat. Up three flights of dimly lit staircases, along a narrow hallway, the children came at last to the door of Auntie's home.

They knocked boldly and the door was opened to them. The children began to chant in unison:

> "Today is Purim
> Tomorrow no more.
> Give me a penny
> And show me the door."

They were greeted with shouts of laughter from all the cousins. Pennies were distributed and in return, one basket

was handed over. Uncle Chaim (Charles) turned to his wife and said very sternly, "Who are these people? Do we know them?" He tweaked the cap on Ella's head and gave Sarah a light slap on her backside. Uncle Chaim was one of Papa's brothers; he had Papa's way of joking with the youngsters.

There were many more houses to visit, so good-bys were said, and the children continued on their way. All afternoon, they went from house to house. To some they brought Purim baskets. To others, only themselves in masquerade. But no matter how they came, they were everywhere welcomed with joy and laughter.

Mama was giving a Purim party. The front-room door was wide open, and the room itself, usually so silent and dark, was now lit up and humming with talk and laughter. All the cousins and uncles and aunts were there: Tanta Rivka and Uncle Chaim with their five children; Uncle Schloimon and Tanta Leah with their three; Uncle Hyman, Tanta Frieda, Tanta Minnie, and many others.

Charlie was there, too, having just as good a time as anyone. He was always at home in Mama's house, even when he was the only gentile present. People liked Charlie, thought Ella, as she watched him. It was easy to like him. He had such grace and charm of manner. How comfortably he chatted away with all the relatives.

Ella wished she could be like that. No matter how much she thought about it beforehand, planning every movement and word, she still became stiff and awkward whenever Charlie was around. She'd find herself saying the silliest things. Maybe it would be different tonight for tonight she'd be in a show. In a show, when you were somebody else, it was easy to be at your best.

Mama's children had arranged a special entertainment for the occasion. They each sang solos and they all sang together.

Ella led an orchestra composed of Charlotte with a frying pan and spatula; Henny with a big spoon and a soup pot; Gertie with two lids for cymbals; and Sarah with a washboard bass viol.

At the end of the show came a special treat. No show was ever over until Ella had sung. She had a beautiful voice and when she sang, the children always said they could feel the walls tremble. She sang a mournful Jewish melody and when she finished there was thunderous applause.

Charlie came over to Ella and took both of her hands in his. "Ella," he said, "that's a fine voice! You sound just like an opera singer."

Ella blushed furiously and her heart pounded. Charlie was holding her hands. Charlie was saying something wonderful about her.

"Charlie!" Papa called out. "Help me pull out the table for the refreshments."

Charlie let go of her hands and left her, and Ella was no longer the great singer. Just plain Ella once more.

Now everybody drank tea out of glasses and ate Haman taschen, Teiglech, nuts, and fruit, till they were full to the top.

The company gradually left. The children went to bed, tired but happy.

Sarah In Trouble

GERTIE WAS GLAD it was twelve o'clock. It had been so lonesome in the house all morning without her sisters. They'll be home any minute now, she thought happily as she helped Mama set the table for lunch. The children would have to go back to school for the afternoon session, but the afternoon never seemed so long. After the lunch dishes had been washed, Mama had a few leisure hours, and unless it was raining, she and Gertie would go out together for a walk.

Henny was the first to arrive. "Gee, I'm hungry," she said as she opened the kitchen door. She sat right down at the table and began to beat a tattoo with her knife and fork.

"Better wash your hands before the others get here," Mama advised.

"Do I have to wash? My hands are clean. Look."

"Clean or not, you get no dinner until you wash your hands."

That settled it, but Henny pouted. She stamped her feet on her way to the kitchen sink and went through the motions of hand washing so quickly she was finished before you could wink your eye.

Today Mama had made rice soup. It gave forth a rich, savory smell of meat and vegetables. Everyone began this first course with relish. That is, everyone but Sarah.

Now Sarah really liked soup. All of Mama's family liked soup. They learned to like it because Mama always served it at the beginning of her dinner.

There was a strict rule about not wasting any food in Mama's house. This rule had been made into a chant by the children:

No soup
No meat.

No meat
No vegetables.

No vegetables
No fruit.

No fruit
No penny.

Sarah, usually so good, must have been feeling especially contrary this morning to think that she could change this rule for her own special benefit. She idly stirred the spoon in her plate of soup and made no attempt to begin eating. When the others had finished, Mama served each one a plate of meat and vegetables, but Sarah got nothing.

"Ma," she said, "you forgot to give me mine."

"You'll get yours as soon as you've finished your soup. You're slow today," Mama replied.

"But I don't want the soup."

Mama only shrugged her shoulders and kept on with her own meal. The other children looked at Sarah in amazement; of course, they thought, she won't persist in not eating this first course. So after a moment they stopped paying any further attention.

Mama served the stewed fruit, but at Sarah's place, the plate of rice soup, now quite cold, still stood untouched.

"Ma, I just don't feel like eating soup today. Can't I have my meat?"

"Of course you can have your meat," Mama assured her, "as soon as the soup is finished."

"But I don't want to eat it."

Mama said nothing.

"I'll choke on it if I eat it," Sarah continued. "I don't want it. I don't want it. I don't want it!" Her voice rose higher with each "I don't want it" until she ended on a shriek.

By this time, Sarah was sure that she hated soup — all soup — but rice soup in particular. Mama had no right to make her eat it. She was more determined than ever not to eat it. She wouldn't give in. She just wouldn't!

Mama looked at Sarah and said very quietly: "If you don't eat your soup, I'm afraid you'll get nothing else for your dinner. You'll have to go back to school without eating."

"So I'll go back without eating, but I won't eat that nasty old rice soup. And I don't care!"

Tears of rage were beginning to appear in Sarah's eyes. The children all felt sorry for her. They knew she was being silly but they could understand. Everybody felt stubborn once in a while. Charlotte whispered, "Aw, give in. Go on, Sarah, give in."

Sarah pushed her away. Deep inside of her a little voice was whispering the same thing, but she couldn't stop now. Some contrary imp had taken hold of her, and she just had to follow along.

Mama distributed the after-lunch pennies. Sarah still sat in her place at the kitchen table.

Papa leaned over and stroked Sarah's hair. "Be a good girl, *Mäusele* (little mouse). Eat your soup. You don't have to eat it all. Just a little and then you can have your nice meat and vegetables." His gentle, soft manner dissolved Sarah in tears, but it was too late now for her to be able to give in. She heard herself saying through a flood of tears.

"I can't eat it! It'll make me sick! I hate it!"

Papa sent an appealing look in Mama's direction. Mama wanted to relent but she knew if she did there would always be trouble with the children in the matter of food and food was too costly to be wasted. So though Mama had to harden herself to continue this struggle with such an unhappy and weeping daughter, she said firmly, "It's just as Papa says. You don't have to eat it all. Just show me that you are really trying to do what is right. This isn't the first time we've had rice soup for lunch and I have seen you eating it many times with a great deal of pleasure. So I'm quite sure that you will not get sick from it."

For answer, Sarah got up from her chair and ran out of the kitchen, down the stairs and into the street. Big sobs welled up in her throat but she choked them back. She couldn't go back to school with a swollen face and red eyes.

All through the afternoon school hours, hunger gnawed at Sarah. She was glad when it was time for dismissal and ran home quickly, eager for food.

Mama was busy ironing. On the kitchen table were the fresh rolls and butter and tea which Mama always served the children after school. Sarah started to pick up a roll but Mama stopped her with the words, "If you're hungry, the rice soup will be warmed up for you in a very few minutes." Mama's voice was quiet but firm.

Oh, how Sarah wanted to say, "All right, Ma, warm it up," but she couldn't. The words refused to come to her lips. She could only burst into tears once more.

She did her homework with the pangs of hunger growing greater by the minute. Every once in a while a tear of self-pity would roll down her cheek.

Mama was equally miserable. She had to keep steeling herself to her firm resolve. Don't be too sorry for her, she told herself. You mustn't. She must learn her lesson. If only she'd take just one spoonful, it would be enough. I'd be able to give in then.

But Sarah wouldn't take even that one spoonful. Finished with her homework, she went to the front room to practice on the piano for half an hour, and then she went outdoors to play until supper time.

Out on the street, her sisters gathered about her sympathetically. She pushed them away rudely, saying, "Leave me alone!" She didn't want their sympathy. If they felt sorry for her, it would only make her feel sorry for herself, and if she became any more sorry for herself than she already was, she'd begin to cry again.

At supper time, the warmed-over rice soup was once again placed in front of Sarah. By this time, it had thickened and formed a lump in the bottom of the plate so that it looked more unattractive than ever. But the hunger inside the little girl could no longer be denied. All the stubbornness melted away and she heard herself saying, "All right, I'll eat some of it."

Then in a flood of tears, tears of self-pity, but tears of relief too, Sarah began to eat the rice soup.

Mama looked at the woebegone figure choking over the soup and she wanted to cry herself. She quickly removed the offensive dish and placed before Sarah a heaping plate of thick, juicy, boiled beef and potatoes. She had deliberately omitted the vegetables tonight so that there need be no further cause for a "must" in eating. Mama knew that she would not have to do any urging for meat and potatoes.

Mama Has Her Hands Full

"ARE'NT YOU GOING to get up this morning?" Ella asked Sarah. It was a school day and usually Sarah was up long before the others.

"I don't feel so good this morning."

"What's the matter? Your throat again?"

"Yes, it hurts when I swallow. My head aches, and my nose feels hot inside."

"You look hot. I'd better call Mama."

When Mama was told she did not get alarmed. Mama was quite used to her children taking their turn on the hospital couch in the kitchen, especially Sarah who spent more time there than her sisters. Mama simply turned the couch into a bed with the aid of white bedclothes and brought her patient in from the bedroom.

Henny looked at Sarah enviously. She hated school and always hoped that something would turn up to prevent her from going. "Heck," she said, "I wish I didn't have to go to school. Ma, won't you need someone to help you now that Sarah is sick?"

"Henny, I'm afraid you'd be more of a hindrance than a help."

Henny went over to Sarah. "Wish I were in your place, lying there so comfortably instead of having to get ready for school."

"I wish you were, too. You only say that because you're hardly ever sick so you don't know how horrid it is. Besides, I like school. I hate to miss it." Sarah's eyes felt hot now too, and a few unhappy tears trickled slowly down her cheeks.

Mama looked at her sick one and then walked over to feel her forehead. It felt burning hot under her cool hand. "Ella," she said at once, "will you stop in at Papa's before you leave for school, and tell him to call Doctor Fuchs?" She wet a face-cloth with cold water, wrung it out, and folding it in a neat oblong, placed it on Sarah's forehead.

After the others had gone, Gertie tried hard in her childish way to amuse Sarah, but Sarah didn't seem to be interested. She kept dozing off.

"Better let her sleep," Mama finally said. "Sleep is the best thing for her right now. You may come and help me with the Passover dishes."

"Ma, why do we call this holiday Passover?"

"Well," said Mama, "the Bible tells us the story about it. Thousands of years ago when the Jewish people lived in Egypt, they were slaves to the Egyptians. Because the Egyptians treated the Jews so cruelly, God punished them in many ways. But the most terrible punishment of all was the Angel of Death. This Angel stopped only in the houses of the Egyptians, killing their first-born sons. He passed over the Jewish houses, and it was this passing over which gave the holiday its name."

"When does Passover begin?"

"In less than a week."

"Oh, goody!" said Gertie. But, oh dear me! thought Mama. Less than a week and so much had to be done to get ready. Throughout the Festival of Passover, which lasts eight days, no bread or leavened foods may be eaten. In the days just before Passover, Jewish people thoroughly clean their homes to remove all traces of such leaven. Even the pots, pans, and dishes have to be changed. Every religious Jewish household has so much kitchenware that it looks like a store. The family must have two sets of dishes for everyday use: one for dairy products and the other for all meat foods; as well as two sets for Passover, to say nothing of special dishes for company use.

Doctor Fuchs was there when the children got home from school. In his booming, cheerful voice, he was telling Sarah to stick out her tongue and say "Aah."

Everybody stood about watching. The examination over, Doctor Fuchs turned to Mama and said gravely, "She's coming down with scarlet fever. I'd better have a look at the others."

"Scarlet fever!" Mama's heart sank. That meant quarantine and isolation. It meant special diets, probably leavened foods, and they were coming into the Passover holidays. How would she manage it? But none of this dismay was noticeable in either her voice or manner. She seemed calm as always as she lined the children up for their examinations.

Henny was first. She seemed all right. So did Gertie and Charlotte. The doctor took much longer when he examined Ella and finally shook his head. "I'm very much afraid this one is ill with it also."

Mama answered very quietly, "It's to be expected. They sleep together."

"You'll have to put these two in bed in a separate room," Doctor Fuchs told Mama. "And try to keep the others away from them. I'll be back in the morning to see how they're doing. Now you're not to worry. They'll come through it all right. Remember, they've got a good doctor."

He laughed loudly at his own joke, trying to cheer Mama, and still laughing, picked up his bag and left.

At last Henny had a perfectly good excuse for staying home from school. But she was far from being delighted. Quarantine! she thought. None of my friends will come near me now. With the two sisters nearest to her age sick, how was she going to amuse herself, she wondered? She couldn't play with babies like Charlotte and Gertie all day long.

Charlotte and Gertie were excited. Scarlet fever in the house! That made them important. Imagine, they were even going to put a sign on the door to let everybody know about it!

But Mama, poor Mama, her heart was heavy even while she moved about so quietly and efficiently. "Keep the sick ones away from the others," the doctor had said. The best way to manage that would be to turn over her bedroom to Ella and

Sarah. She'd sleep in the room with them. Sick children often needed their mother during the long nights. She could use the cot which was kept ready for just such emergencies. Papa could be put up on the kitchen couch, or if he preferred, in Ella's and Sarah's bed in the children's room.

She prepared the bedroom that would be the sick room for many weeks to come. Then changing into a clean house dress, she put her patients to bed and made them as comfortable as possible. Then she removed her sickroom uniform and returned to the kitchen.

"You all heard what the doctor said," Mama said to her other girls. "You must never go into the bedroom where Ella and Sarah now are. I don't want the rest of you getting sick too. Henny, please take this prescription to the drugstore. Wait until he prepares the medicine and then bring it back. Stop in at Papa's and tell him the children have Scarlet Fever. As for you, Charlotte and Gertie, help me put these dishes back into the barrel. They'll have to stay there until the last minute."

"Ma," asked Charlotte, "will we have the Seder nights anyway?"

"Yes, of course," Mama replied.

Charlotte was thinking about the ceremonial feasts which

118

are held on the first two nights of the Passover festival. At these feasts, through reading parts of the Bible, singing religious songs, and eating special, meaningful foods, the Jews once again relive the days spent in Egypt so many thousands of years ago.

"Will Ella and Sarah be all better by then?" Gertie asked.

"No, I don't think so. Of course, they'll be feeling much better," her mother added quickly, "but they'll still have to stay in bed."

That night, Mama awoke from a deep, exhausted sleep to the sound of crying. Fully awake at once, as she always was when one of the children needed her, she recognized the voice as Sarah's. "Don't cry," Mama said soothingly. "I'm here."

"Make it stop, make it stop!" Sarah cried.

"Yes," Mama replied, "I'll make it stop." No use to argue with a feverish child that there was nothing to stop.

Ella, meanwhile, sat up in bed, very unhappy. "She's delirious, isn't she, Mama?"

"Yes, she probably had a bad dream. She'll quiet down in a minute."

"I had a bad dream! A bad dream!" Sarah's sobbing was growing quieter. "Something was growing big, very big, and

I couldn't stop it no matter how much I tried. I looked at my fingers and they got all swollen up. And my face kept getting fatter and fatter all the time. I felt like I was going to burst. Then I got very frightened and called you."

"Well, I'm here now so there's nothing for you to be frightened about. Try to go back to sleep and I'll sit right here beside you to chase away the bad dreams." And so through the stillness of the night, Mama sat at the bedside with Sarah's hand in hers until both children were again asleep. Then, quietly removing Sarah's hand, she crept back to her own bed.

In the morning both children seemed a bit better though Sarah's face was rapidly turning as red as a beet. Ella thought she looked very funny until a few spots came out on her own forehead and around her ears.

A little later, a man from the Board of Health appeared and stayed just long enough to put a quarantine sign on the outside of the kitchen door. Charlotte and Gertie kept going outside to gaze with awe at the sign. "It makes our house look like it belongs to somebody else, doesn't it?" Charlotte said.

That afternoon there was a knock on the door. "Who is it?" Mama called out.

"It's me, Charlie," came the answer. "It's all right. You

can open the door. I won't come in. I just ran up for a little chat."

Mama came out to talk with Charlie.

"How are Ella and Sarah?" he asked.

"Sarah was pretty sick last night," Mama said.

"It's hard on you," Charlie said, sympathetically. "Is there something I can do? Can I get you anything from the stores?"

"Thanks, Charlie, but Papa has already done the shopping for me today."

"Well — I brought a little something for the patients to keep them busy. See that little package in the corner near the door? Yes, that's it," he said as Mama picked up the small parcel. "And, Mama, take it easy, will you?"

The sick ones were pleased with their present — two little blackboards, an eraser, and a box of colored chalk.

"Now when we feel better we can write on the blackboard — just like in school," said Sarah.

"Isn't Charlie kind and thoughtful?" said Ella.

The next three days went by quickly enough. The doctor came in the mornings, examined the sick ones, joked with the others, and was gone. In the daytime, Sarah would be lively and gay and she and Ella would enjoy themselves. But when night came, her fever would mount and she would call for Mama. Mama spent three more sleepless nights.

On the fourth morning, Mama reminded the children at breakfast, "Passover begins this evening."

Mama was ready. Her house was in order and the Passover dishes were clean. Mr. Basch, the grocer, had piled up outside the door many packages, including special Passover foods.

The sick ones were getting better. The rash on their faces and bodies was beginning to fade. It really seemed as if everything was going to be all right after all.

That afternoon, Charlotte and Gertie were sitting on the kitchen couch, drawing funny pictures. Both little girls had been unusually quiet all day, and if Mama had not been so busy, she would have noticed and wondered about it. But she had not noticed and Charlotte's words found her unprepared. "Ma, I feel sort of funny. My throat hurts."

And as if that were not enough, Gertie spoke up too. "My throat doesn't hurt but I feel tired."

"Wouldn't it be funny if we got scarlet fever, too?" said Charlotte. "Our house would be a regular hospital house."

Funny, thought Mama. Funny indeed! But to the children she said only, "We'll have Doctor Fuchs take a look at you when he comes. I'm expecting him any minute."

Doctor Fuchs came and looked. There was no doubt about it. Mama had two more cases of scarlet fever on her hands. Henny was sent for Papa. When he came, the "hospital room" was fixed up so that it could accommodate four patients, and Charlotte and Gertie were put to bed. Ella and Sarah hailed the newcomers joyfully.

But Henny stamped up and down the kitchen angrily. Why did she alone have to be well? Now there'd be nobody for her to play with. "I want to be sick too," she yelled.

"Hush, you foolish child," Mama and Papa told her. "Do you think it's pleasant to be feeling ill?"

The children felt sorry for Henny. "She must be awfully lonesome," Ella said sympathetically. She leaned back against her pillow with a sigh of contentment.

It was the first Seder night. How empty and lonely the table looked with its setting for only three on this night when the poor, the friends, and the relatives were wont to be the invited guests! The shiny crystal goblets were filled with wine, a large goblet for Papa, a medium-sized one for Mama, and a little one for Henny. A clean white napkin covered the Seder platter which Papa had arranged earlier. The platter held three pieces of matzoth which stood for unity (for all Jews should be brotherly). In the upper right-hand corner of this platter, Papa had placed the paschal lamb (a shank bone) and in the upper left-hand corner, a roasted egg, both symbols of the sacrifices offered up by the Jews in ancient times on this holy day. In the center of the platter was the horse-radish (bitter herb); in the lower right-hand corner, in a small dish, was a mixture of ground nuts, apple, and wine to resemble the clay and bricks which the Jews had made for the Pharaoh in Egypt many thousands of years ago. In the lower left-hand corner lay a sprig of parsley, symbol of springtime and of hope.

Papa's Morris chair and the leather couch were pulled up close to the table and piled high with cushions, for on this night Mama and Papa would recline as King and Queen while they ate their meal.

No need to worry tonight about having enough Haggadahs to go around. Haggadahs are the books which date back about two thousand years and tell the story of Passover. Mama's were written in Hebrew and English so that the children were able to follow the story as it was intoned by Papa. The little books were so full of droll pictures that even Gertie had always found pleasure in looking through them.

The oldest and greatest of Jewish festivals was about to begin with this strange and beautiful ceremony, and in Mama's house, four sick little girls wept because they could not take full part in it.

Papa put on his kittel just as in ancient times when the festive clothing of the Jews had always been white. He stood

for a moment in the open doorway of the bedroom so that the little ones might see him in all his splendor.

"Don't cry," he told them. "We shall keep the door open throughout the services. I shall read loudly so you will be able to hear me. Join in when you can."

The sick ones dried their eyes, determining to listen carefully so that they might hear everything even if they couldn't see.

Hands were washed. The prayer over the wine was said, and the wine sipped. Papa refilled the glasses. Next he handed out small twigs of parsley which the three dipped in salt water and ate. The salt water was in memory of the tears the Jews had shed when they had been slaves in Egypt. Papa broke the middle piece of matzoth and put a large piece away between the pillows on his chair. Every other Seder, the children had watched him attentively at this point, for the child who could succeed in removing this hidden piece of matzoth without Papa's discovering it until the end of the Seder would receive as her reward whatever gift she chose to ask for. Papa had always had difficulty in determining who the thief was but tonight there would be no cause for doubt.

The Haggadahs were open and Papa began to chant in

Hebrew: "All who are hungry, come and feast; all who have no Seder of their own, come and join . . ."

They soon reached that part of the ceremony where the youngest son in the family, or in the absence of a son, the youngest daughter, asks the father four questions which call for an explanation of the festival. For weeks, Gertie had been rehearsing her part. Now she wasn't even at the table to say it. Papa waited and soon from the bedroom came the sound of the childish voice singing the words hesitantly, "Father, why is this night so different from other nights?"

When she had finished, Papa began reading swiftly. Only his voice chanted aloud, whereas on other Seder nights the table hummed loudly with the chanting of all the invited guests.

The services continued. Page after page was turned as Papa chanted until finally the Haggadahs were laid aside. The meal was about to begin. First came a second cup of wine. Once again hands were washed. Papa gave his table companions a bit of matzoth, and a benediction was recited by the three. Next the portions of bitter herbs were eaten. Mama brought a bowl full of hard-boiled eggs to the table, for eggs signified life and health. They were dipped into the salt water and then eaten. After this first course came chicken soup with matzoth balls (dumplings made of matzoth flour), chicken, vegetables, and stewed fruit.

When the meal was over, Papa looked for his afikomen (the hidden piece of matzoth). It was gone. Gertie cried out from the bedroom, "I wanted to steal the afikomen. I never had a chance before. Everybody promised they'd let me tonight. Now I won't get a present."

"Never mind, Gertie," Henny called out in answer. "I've got it, and I'm not going to give it back to Papa unless he promises to give us both something."

Papa's eyes twinkled merrily. "It looks like I'm being held up. Well, what do I have to offer you in exchange for that afikomen?"

"I want a little washtub and a little washboard so I can wash my dolly's clothes," Gertie answered at once.

"Good enough," Papa said. "How about you, Henny?"

"Oh, I'll take a nickel. Now do you solemnly promise to give us both what we asked for?"

Papa promised and Henny handed over the afikomen. Papa broke off a piece for each one to be eaten as dessert, just as in the old days a piece of the paschal lamb was given to each person who came to the Temple.

And now it was time to open the door for the Prophet Elijah who some day will announce the coming of the Jewish Messiah. A glass of wine had been poured for him, for it is told that he visits every home on the Seder night. The door was opened to allow him to enter so that he might partake of the wine. Always the children would watch the door intently, hopeful that they might see the Prophet or at least hear the rush of his wings as he flew in. Somehow they never saw, they never heard, but they were sure, every time, that the glass held a little less than it did before the door was opened.

"Papa," they called out, "is there less in the glass?"

"Yes," Papa replied, "I can see he was here." And Henny echoed, "Yes, he was here."

It was late. The sick ones were tired so they dispensed with the usual singing of folk songs. Mama and Henny cleared away quickly and the first Seder night was over.

After that the family became accustomed to the idea of being completely alone. For Mama the days were so work-filled, there was no time for thought. She even stopped trying to prevent Henny from catching scarlet fever. It was a useless effort because Henny was in the bedroom every time Mama's back was turned. Then Doctor Fuchs felt that Henny was not susceptible to the disease or she would have come down with it long ago.

Mama's only contact with people outside of her own family was by way of the window. Every afternoon at the same time, the doorbell would ring. Mama would rush to the front-room window to greet the relative who had that day come to call.

Every few days, too, would come the knock on the door which meant that Charlie was there. He would question Mama about the children's condition and always he would leave "a little something" for them. Sometimes it was a page of funny pictures, or a little note so amusing it set them off in gales of laughter. Once he left red cherry hearts, a candy delight the children all dearly loved. Occasionally some small toy or game would be in the surprise package. The children looked forward to Charlie's presents, and Mama could not get over his constant consideration for her little family.

"Charlie," she said, "I've never known a kinder person. The children are so grateful. They tell me to thank you over and over again. We all wish we knew how to repay you."

"But it's nothing, Mama — really," he answered in embarrassment. "I just want the kids to be happy."

"If you could only see how happy you make them, Charlie."

"That's fine," he answered and ran quickly down the stairs.

There was also a memorable day when the postman brought a heavy brown envelope addressed to all the children. They couldn't quite believe it was for them. Nobody had ever sent them anything through the mails before. Finally, Ella broke the seal and took out a brand new copy of the St. Nicholas magazine. There was a note pinned to it which she read aloud.

It was from Miss Allen and she told them to hurry up and get well; she missed seeing their happy faces.

"She's so nice," Sarah said when the note was read. "I just love her."

"We all love her," said Ella, and everyone agreed.

When Passover was through, things were not so difficult for Mama and her girls. Still, when at last the day for fumigating the apartment arrived, it was a happy and thankful group that hailed the inspector from the Board of Health.

Fourth of July

"SUCH A NICE FLAG," said Gertie, as she put her hand out gingerly to touch the red-white-and-blue bunting which lay rolled up on the kitchen couch.

Henny picked it up and began to unroll it.

"Put it down," ordered Papa. "I don't want the American flag on the floor."

Henny was glad to obey; the flagpole Papa had made was heavy. "Bet you don't know what day this is," she said to Gertie.

It was true. Gertie didn't know. Usually Papa left for his shop before the children awoke. But here he was in the kitchen with them. It wasn't the Sabbath. Well then, it must be a holiday. "I do, too," she told Henny triumphantly, "It's a holiday."

"Everybody knows it's a holiday," Henny said. "But what holiday? Don't you remember from last year?"

"Let her alone," Mama said. "She's too little to remember last year." Turning to Gertie, she explained. "It's the Fourth of July."

"Fourth of July?" Gertie repeated questioningly.

"Independence Day," Ella answered. "It's a holiday all over the country."

Papa carried the flag carefully into the front room so it could be displayed from a window overlooking the street. Gertie and Charlotte looked out the window and noticed that almost all the neighbors, up and down the street, had hung out flags also.

Ella was grating potatoes for potato kugel. After a while her right arm was beginning to ache. "Mama," she asked, "how many kugels are you making?"

"One, but it's got to be a big one. Charlie's staying for supper and you know how he loves potato kugel."

Since it was for Charlie, Ella didn't care how much her arm ached. I'll have to hurry if I want to do my hair again before he gets here, she decided, and fell to grating busily.

As soon as the task was done, she ran into the bedroom.

She unbraided her thick black hair and brushed it till it lay shiny and silken against her small head. She tied the front ends back with a wide pink bow to match her dress, then studied herself in the mirror. Yes, this made her look much more grown-up.

It wasn't any too soon, for there was a knock on the kitchen door and in walked Charlie with a large box in his hand. The children gathered around him. They knew the package must be for them because he kept pulling it out of their reach and holding it high above their heads, teasingly. Only Ella stood apart. She felt she was getting too big for such childish romping, and besides, her hair might get mussed.

"Take these young scamps off me, Mama," he begged. "They're tearing me apart." But all the while he was laughing as if he didn't really want them to leave him alone. Finally he thrust the box into Ella's hands. "Here you are!" The children left Charlie and surrounded Ella instead.

Charlie sat down on the couch. He took off his straw hat and wiped the inside band with his pocket handkerchief. "Phew!" he exclaimed, rubbing his hand over the red ring on his forehead the tight hatband had made.

Meanwhile the children were shouting, "Let's see, Ella.

What's in it?" and trying to poke their heads into the box all at the same time.

"Wait a minute!" Ella said. "You're tearing the box." She put it down on the kitchen table and took off the cover. Inside was an assortment of small red tubes with little wicks attached.

"Red candles!" cried Gertie.

"Firecrackers!" her sisters all yelled. "Ooh — let's shoot them off right away!"

"Let's get the matches!" Henny flew to the shelf above the kitchen stove where they were kept.

"Hold on there!" Charlie called out warningly. "I'll take those." And his long legs strode across the kitchen floor to rescue the matches. "We can't shoot off firecrackers in the house. Get the box, Ella, and I'll see you all downstairs." He was out the kitchen door like a shot, and the children tumbled over each other in their haste to catch up with him.

The streets were full of excitement. Everybody was expressing their joy in freedom today. From tenement house windows and from store fronts flew American flags of all sizes. The air was filled with the clang of cowbells and the blasts of horns. Youngsters in small groups yelled and hopped up and down as they waited with bated breath for their firecrackers to explode. At times the noise was deafening! And now Mama's children were to add their share to the general hubbub.

➤ "Firecrackers are a lot of fun, but they can be dangerous," cautioned Charlie. "So we will have to be careful. I was careless once when I was a little boy and I burnt my hands badly."

"Tell us about it, Charlie," said Ella eagerly.

"Well, it was a long time ago. I must have been about Charlotte's age. You should have seen me then. I was dressed in white pants and white blouse with a blue-striped sailor collar."

"I bet you looked cute," Henny said.

"I suppose so," Charlie smiled at the memory. "We had just moved to a summer cottage at the seashore. It was a pleasant place, with tall trees shading the front lawn. There were lots of flowers, too. And there was always a fresh, clean breeze from the ocean." Charlie's voice faded away for a moment. He half closed his eyes as if trying to recall the scene.

"Father and I were shooting off firecrackers and Mother watched us from the front porch. Father warned me to be careful but I paid no attention. I held the lighted firecracker in my hand and watched the bright flame. The next second, it exploded in my hands.

"Father rushed me to the kitchen and put oil on my burnt fingers. I ran to Mother and she took me in her arms. I cried, and cried . . ."

Charlie seemed to have forgotten the children. He stopped talking and looked off into the distance.

Ella watched Charlie, trying to imagine him as a small boy. But her sisters were tugging at his elbow. "Charlie," they shouted. He shook himself as if to get free of his memory. He was back on the East Side now — back to the narrow, smelly streets, teeming with people.

"Charlie, did it hurt?" Gertie asked.

"Did what hurt?"

"When you burnt your hand."

Charlie smiled down at Gertie so full of concern for him. "Uh — yes, it hurt, but not too much. Come on — let's shoot off the first one."

Charlie lit the firecrackers and threw them away from the little group. The girls stood fascinated, holding their hands to their ears and jumping when the firecrackers exploded.

When the firecrackers were all gone, Mama called them up for supper.

What a wonderful meal it was! Five pairs of eyes shone

both from the excitement of the firecrackers and the pleasure of having Charlie there for supper.

"Charlie," said Mama as she served the meat course, "I've made one of your favorite dishes today."

"Oh boy! Potato pudding, I bet!"

Mama took the kugel out of the oven and bore it triumphantly to the table. It looked very festive in all its crusty, brown deliciousness on Mama's best company platter. She set it down right before Charlie. "All for me?" Charlie looked at the children. "Too bad, kids, there won't be any for you."

"Well," Mama laughed, "if you have a mind to be generous, you might give us each a small portion."

"M-mm!" Charlie said, after he had finished his third helping. "It surely tasted wonderful, but I just can't eat another mouthful."

"When you get married, Charlie," Mama told him, "you send your wife to me and I'll give her the recipe."

"I will," said Charlie, "if I ever have a wife."

Somehow Mama must have said the wrong thing, for the laughter had gone from Charlie's face. Ella twisted the napkin in her hands and looked at him unhappily. There was an awkward silence.

All at once the silence was broken. From the street there arose the eerie shriek of whistles, the clanging of bells and the pounding of hoofs.

"Fire engines!" everybody yelled and jumped up from their chairs to rush madly to the front-room windows.

They were just in time to see four gray horses gallop by, pulling the fire engine. The fire house dog ran beside the lead horses, barking furiously. Close on the engine came a long red hook-and-ladder truck. The firemen clung perilously to their perches as the wagons rounded the corner. People in the gutters scrambled to get out of the way, and little boys raced excitedly in a vain attempt to keep up with the horses.

"If I were a boy," said Henny, "that's what I would want to be — a fireman!"

"If you were a boy . . ." Papa began and stopped. If only at least one child had been a boy, he thought. But which one? He smiled to himself. He couldn't possibly imagine life without any one of his five girls.

". . . you'd be too much for one Mama to manage," Mama finished for him.

Behind them all, Gertie's little voice said timidly, "Are they gone, Charlie?"

Charlie turned to the small figure. Her eyes were big and scared-looking. He picked the little girl up.

"What's the matter?" he asked. "Afraid of the fire-engines?"

"I don't like that noise," Gertie said. "It scares me!"

"I don't like that noise, either," said Mama. "It means the bonfires have started already. The fire department is going to have a busy night putting them out.

"The tar on the streets melts," added Papa, "and the cobblestones get loose. Then the city has a job to repair the damage."

"I wish we could see the bonfires," Henny said.

"Oh, no!" Mama was firm. "I don't want any of you children near a fire."

Charlie looked at the downcast faces. "Never mind," he said. "I'll show you something even better than a bonfire. Meet me downstairs in fifteen minutes — Papa and Mama, too." He was gone before anyone could say a word.

The time passed slowly for the impatient children. What could be better than a bonfire, they asked each other. They were consumed with curiosity. When finally Charlie reappeared with an even bigger box this time, they fell upon him like a bunch of puppy dogs.

"Another box, Charlie!" everyone shouted.

"Uh-huh," Charlie told them. "It's a surprise."

"He's full of surprises today," Ella said admiringly.

"Charlie, what did you get now?" exclaimed Mama. "You already bought them firecrackers. You shouldn't be throwing your money around like this."

"That's Charlie," Papa said. "Today a millionaire, tomorrow he won't have a nickel in his pocket."

Charlie laughed. "Who'll I save my money for?"

He opened the box and pulled out something that looked like the sawed-off end of a broomstick. "See, kids! This is a Roman candle. There's one for each, but I'll shoot them off."

He held the stick upright in his left hand and lit the fuse with the other. As he waved it slowly in a circular motion, it began to give out sparks. "Now watch! Here she goes!"

ZOOM! A ball of white fire shot up towards the rooftops. ZOOM! A red ball followed a moment later. ZOOM! Out came a yellow. ZOOM! Last of all, a green!

Faces uplifted in awed wonder, the astonished children followed the flight of the globes of flame against the dark sky. Each glowing ball hung there for a moment like a glittering star, and then disappeared.

141

"Just look at all the colors!" cried Charlotte.

Even Papa and Mama were thrilled. "Something marvelous!" exclaimed Papa.

"Here goes another!" cried Charlie.

Once again the magical colors streamed heavenward. Soon around the family there gathered an ever-increasing audience. Here was a display they could watch for nothing. From all sides the neighbors and their children came running. From tenement house windows, a multitude of heads stretched forth over the sills to gape at the rare treat. Mama's children felt proud because it was their Charlie who was giving everybody such a good time.

"That's all!" said Charlie, as the children watched the last flicker of the last Roman candle. "The box is empty. The show is over."

The bystanders gradually drifted away. The little girls were tired, and there wasn't a word of protest when Mama announced, "Upstairs, children. It's way past your bedtime."

"What a day!" cried Henny as the family started up the stairs.

"Yes," said Mama, "thanks to our Charlie, we've had enough excitement to last a year."

143

After Mama and the girls had gone upstairs, Papa and Charlie sat on the steps and talked. They talked a long time.

When Papa came upstairs at last the girls were asleep, all but Ella. She lay beside Sarah, thinking about all the wonderful fun they had had with Charlie.

Ella heard Papa draw up a chair at the open window beside Mama's. She heard him say:

"I guess Charlie was homesick or lonesome or something tonight. The good time he had with the children made him think of his home, I suppose. Anyway he talked a lot about himself."

Ella lifted herself up on her elbows so she could hear everything.

"It seems that Charlie quarreled with his parents about a girl he wanted to marry. They wanted him to marry another girl.

"Charlie's girl learned that his parents opposed their marriage, and she just went away. Charlie looked for her everywhere he could think of, but he couldn't find a trace of her. She was an orphan and he didn't know any of her people."

Ella heard Mama's sympathetic "Tck, tck," and her own heart was heavy as lead.

"It ruined Charlie's life," Papa went on. "When he lost his girl, he lost interest in everything. He was very angry at his parents, and left home. He gave up his career, he dropped his friends, his old life — even his old name. His full name is Herbert Charles Graham.

"But he's never stopped trying to find the girl. All those weeks when he stays away from the shop, he is out looking for her. He's even advertised in the papers, but he has never had an answer.

"That's why he lives down here. The life of the people here is so different from what he knew before. Here he finds it easier to forget. . . ."

Papa's voice died away, and he and Mama sat in silent thought. Then to their ears came the sound of muffled weeping. Mama looked at Papa in surprise. She rose and went into the other room.

Ella's face was buried in her damp pillow; she was trying to stop but the sobs grew heavier instead.

"Come, come, my darling," Mama said tenderly. "Why do you cry so hard?"

"It's — so — s-sad," Ella said in muffled tones. "P-poor — Charlie!"

"Come with me," Mama said kindly. "We will talk out here where we won't wake the others."

Her head in Mama's lap and her hand in Papa's, Ella told how she had lain awake and couldn't help but hear the story. She didn't say that she had been crying too at the mere thought of her idol Charlie's having a sweetheart.

"It is all very sad," Mama agreed, smoothing her eldest's dark head. "It is always very sad when parents and children quarrel."

"Maybe it will all come out right some day," Papa said hopefully. "Anyway, I think it helped Charlie to talk about it." Papa sighed. He really felt saddened over Charlie's unhappiness, for Charlie was very close to Papa, almost like a brother — or a son.

"Can you sleep now, Ella?" Mama asked. "You must try. It is late."

"All right, Mama. I'll go back to bed."

Ella crawled in beside Sarah. Back in bed, however, the tears fell anew — tears for Charlie's unhappiness, tears for herself, for now she knew that Charlie was not really her Charlie. His heart belonged to somebody else.

Family Outing

"Aren't we lucky it isn't raining," declared Henny.

"We certainly are," Sarah agreed.

"And who cares if it is hot!" sang out Charlotte.

Ella said, "The hotter, the better!"

It had been hot for more than a week — terribly, unbelievably hot. All day the sun had blazed on a sweltering city, and at night many of the East Siders escaped from the stifling air of their boxlike flats to sleep on fire escapes and rooftops. In Mama's house the bedrooms were unbearable. The mattresses were removed from the beds and laid out on the floor of the front room. But that had offered little relief. For hours each night, the family tossed about in sleepless discomfort.

Mama finally decided that no matter how much trouble it might mean for her, the children would have to be taken away from the city even if it were for only one day. "If it's as hot as this tomorrow, we shall go to the beach," she told the children.

Now it was tomorrow. It had not rained, and the heat was as intense as ever. In Mama's house there was great excitement. Ella was helping to wrap up the lunch in clean, white shoeboxes. Sarah was busy buttoning Gertie up the back. "Stand still," she demanded, "you wiggle like a fish."

As usual when things were stirring, Charlotte sat lost in thought. One high-buttoned shoe was in her hand, the other lay on the floor beside her. Mama looked up from the lunch wrapping and noticed her. "Dreamer! Wake up!" She shook Charlotte lightly on the shoulder. "Do you want to be left behind?" That brought Charlotte back to the everyday world at once.

When at last everything was ready, there were so many parcels that each child had to carry one. They set out for the streetcar which would take them to the beach.

Though it was early in the morning, the car depot was already full to overflowing with the noisy, pushing, excited throng. The children clung tightly to Mama and to each other

148

as they were hustled up the stairs of the car and into their seats. They were lucky to get seats even though they were wedged together in a space meant for half their number. Before the car pulled away from the station, Mama counted her young ones to make sure she had them all with her.

A rush of warm air began to blow in their faces as the car started to move and all settled down for the long, long ride.

Ella was wedged into a corner next to Mama. She said softly, "What's happening to Charlie, Mama?"

"Nothing," Mama answered. "He's feeling pretty hopeless these days, Papa says. Papa feels very bad too, because he's so fond of Charlie."

Ella sat quietly thinking about Charlie. After the first shock of discovering about his sweetheart, Ella's thoughts had been captivated with the romance, imagining various happy endings to the affair. Soon she had a mental picture of Charlie's girl; she was lovely, of course, and filled with the highest ideals; kind and gentle — but proud and high-spirited, too. Some day Charlie would be riding on a streetcar — just like this — and a girl would get on, a beautiful golden-haired girl, beautifully dressed; Charlie would look once, then twice — then he would take her in his arms. . . .

"Look — Coney Is-land," Charlotte said, rousing Ella from her dreams. She pronounced it just like that. Ella and Henny laughed. "Coney Island, you mean. You don't sound the *s* in the word island."

Coney Is-land or Coney Island, they were here at last. "Thank goodness!" Mama exclaimed, gathering up her children and bundles. She counted her brood again. They were all still with her.

At the City Bath Houses, Ella, Henny, and Sarah undressed in one locker, while Mama shared another with Charlotte and Gertie. They got into their bathing suits quickly, took the sweaters, the lunch, and their bathhouse keys and went at once to the hot, sandy beach. It wasn't so easy to find a place in which to settle themselves and their belongings. The beaches were crowded with other mamas who had sought relief for their children. But finally, when they had walked a few beach blocks away from the bathhouse, a suitable spot was found. The children dropped their bundles and raced madly down to the water's edge.

"Ooh, it's cold," said Sarah as the water lapped at her toes.

"Aw, come on! Let's get wet all over quickly," suggested Henny. "Then we won't mind it so much."

The children agreed that this was the best plan. They stepped back to where the waves did not reach, then joining hands, they ran without stopping into the ocean until the water came up to Gertie's chest. "Ready, set, go!" Ella counted. Down they splashed, straight into the heart of a wave. Wet all over, they stood up spluttering.

"It's hard to believe now that it's terribly hot in the city," Ella said.

"Uh-huh," Charlotte agreed. "I'm glad Mama brought us here."

They splashed about happily. They formed a circle and played Ring-Around-The-Rosy. Mama had remembered to bring a ball, and they tossed it back and forth to one another. They ducked through some waves and rode on the backs of others. They had a glorious time.

Mama could hardly get them out. They stayed in the water till their lips got blue and their bodies shivered with the thorough chilling. That was when the sweaters came in handy. Mama spread the lunch and to the famished children, the simple food tasted wonderful. There were bread-and-butter sandwiches, Mama's kind, a slice of sour rye bread placed against a slice of pumpernickel. With these, they ate hard-boiled eggs and whole tomatoes sprinkled liberally with salt. For herself Mama had brought limburger sandwiches. The children found it hard to believe that they tasted better than they smelled.

"Ocean bathing certainly gives you children an appetite," Mama remarked as she watched the shoeboxes becoming empty one by one.

At the end, Mama had a wonderful surprise — store-bought cakes! Not just plain cakes like the ones Mama baked at home for the Sabbath, but fancy ones with icing — chocolate and vanilla!

When lunch was over, Mama would not let them go back into the water for an hour. So they spent the time playing in the sand. They built tunnels with the aid of sea-shell scoops, they made mud pies, and buried one another in the sand, up to their necks.

Suddenly Henny looked up and said, "Ma, are we going to Playland, today?"

"Oh, are we, Ma? Are we?" the others echoed eagerly.

Mama hesitated before answering. The section where the colorful booths and sideshows were located was a good distance away. She was already tired, and it would be quite a job to lead five young ones through the crowds along the boardwalk. But the children's faces were so pleading. They seldom had such treats. She was always so busy at home and there was very little extra money. She couldn't say no. After all they just wanted to see the sights, and that wouldn't cost any money. "All right," she said finally, and the children squealed with delight.

"But," Mama continued, "we will have to hurry. We must get back to the cars early in order to avoid the crowds. So just go into the water once, wash the sand off your bodies and bathing suits and then we'll get dressed as quickly as we can."

It is amazing, thought Mama, how quickly the girls can do things when they have something to look forward to. In no time at all they were proceeding towards what seemed to the children to be fairyland. Henny, Ella and Sarah walked directly in front of Mama so she could keep her eyes on them while she held Gertie by one hand and Charlotte by the other.

It was exciting walking along the boardwalk. Their feet went *clippety-clop* on the wooden boards. They rubbed shoulders with hundreds of other folk also bent on sightseeing. In the distance they could see the big scenic railway, its dizzying up-and-down hills circling round and round ever higher and higher up in the sky.

"Gosh, I wouldn't want to go on one of these, would you?" Charlotte asked of Gertie.

"Not me!" replied Gertie.

"I would! I'd like to go up right now!" Henny said, staring skyward with shining, excited eyes.

"You're none of you going. It's much too dangerous. So you might just as well stop thinking about it." Mama promptly ended that discussion.

The first booths were already in view. Their owners leaned over the counters and barked loudly to the crowds. "Get your hot dogs here!" "Peanuts and cracker jack!" "Ice cream, lady?" "Salt water taffy!" "Step right up and get a jelly apple, sister!"

They came upon shooting galleries where wonderful prizes were offered to those who were good shots. They passed booths where games of chance could be played. Outside of small curtained stalls stood gypsy ladies in numerous skirts of many colors, all eager to tell fortunes for just a few pennies. Mama and the girls made slow progress along the boardwalk for they stopped to stare at everything.

Soon above the noise, they could hear jolly organ music. That meant they were near the carousel. They quickened their pace for they loved the whirling horses so splendid in their shiny colors. When they had reached it, they stood still and watched wistfully while other little girls and boys climbed aboard the platform to be lifted up to the backs of these most beautiful animals. They did not ask Mama to let them ride. They knew there was no money to spare for such luxuries. It was a long time before they consented to move. Gathering them together Mama checked off rapidly: "Ella, Henny, Sarah, Charlotte, and Gertie — all here."

"Hurry, hurry, hurry!" urged the loud voice of a barker who stood before a large tent. "Step inside, folks, and you will see the wonders of the world, all for the price of only one dime. You will see the Tallest Man and the Shortest Little Lady in the whole world! We will show you the Tattooed Lady and the Wild Man From Borneo. These and many, many others. All you have to pay is ten cents. Ten cents!"

The little girls gazed in awe at the large, bright paintings of the wonders which were posted on billboards high above the entrance. To their delight, one of the freaks emerged from inside the tent to be gaped at by the audience. It was The Bearded Lady. Sarah took one look and said out loud, "Gosh, her beard is even longer than Uncle Schloimon's." Her sisters all tittered, and so did those about her who had heard.

They would have stayed there forever, but Mama reminded them that it was getting late and there wasn't much time left for sightseeing.

It was the Ferris Wheel which next caught their attention. It seemed a bit frightening to the children as they craned their necks upward to the top of the circle the wheel made. Suddenly they heard a startled cry from Mama, "Where's Henny?"

"Why, she was right here beside me," Ella said.

Mama scanned the crowds frantically and called aloud, "Henny! Henny!" But there was no answer. She looked in all directions but it was next to impossible to see anyone in the shifting masses of people.

157

Mama's breathing became rapid with anxiety. The thing she had dreaded all day had actually happened: one of her little ones was lost. Thank God, she thought to herself, that we're not on the beach or I might imagine she's drowned. Where should she look for her? Where first?

"Ella," Mama said, "you're to stay here with the children. Don't move from this spot until I return. I'm going ahead a little way. Perhaps Henny went on faster than we did. If, however, she should happen to come by here while I'm gone, don't come after me. Just keep her here with you until I get back."

Mama went on ahead walking rapidly, her eyes ever searching the passing throngs. She stopped at each booth and hunted through the crowds. Just a little while ago her back had ached with tiredness. So had her feet, but now she had completely forgotten about these aches in her great anxiety for her "wild one." Her throat felt tight with worry and unshed tears. In desperation she began to ask people if they had seen a little girl with blonde curls who was lost. But though all were sympathetic, they could give no answer to her question.

When Mama got back to the children, there was still no Henny. Ella had moved the group over a little to where a bench had been vacated. Onto this bench Mama sank wearily.

Gertie had begun to cry so Mama took her on her lap and soothed her gently.

Ella looked at Mama's tired face and said, "Look, Ma, I'll go back to that place where all the queer people were being shown. I bet she's still standing there. I'll look for her very carefully."

Mama nodded her head in agreement so Ella started off. As soon as she reached the tent that had held their attention for so long, she began a thorough search but it was of no use. There was no sign of the lost one. With a heavy heart she had just about decided to return to Mama and the girls when the loud voice of the barker checked her. "Say, sister, lookin' for somethin'?"

"Yes," she answered, "my sister."

The audience burst out laughing. They thought it was some sort of joke. But Ella's tears began to flow and that was no joke. The crowd soon realized that a child really was lost. They circled about Ella, plying her with questions. "What does she look like?" "How tall is she?" "How long ago was she here?" Ella answered as best she could.

It was the barker who finally suggested, "Say, sister, why don't you try the police station? There's one just a few blocks from here. That's where they always take the lost kids. I'll bet you anythin' your sister's there right now."

Everybody thought the suggestion was excellent, and Ella felt her spirits lifting in hope. "I'll go back and tell my mama first," she said, wiping the tears away from her eyes with the back of her hand. "She and my sisters are waiting a little way from here. We'll go to the police station together."

She fairly flew on the way back to Mama and the children. Breathlessly she explained what the barker had said. They all left the boardwalk and asked the first policeman they met the way to the station house. When he heard what had happened, he led them there himself.

And there inside the station house, seated on a bench among a number of weepy, disheveled children, was a smiling little girl with blonde curls. She was swinging her feet and munching away in complete rapture on an enormous chocolate ice-cream cone. In her lap lay a thick bar of peanut candy and a red lollipop. She looked up from her ice cream for a moment and saw Mama and the children. "Oh, hello!" she called out cheerily and went right back to her munching.

Mama was too relieved to be able to scold her. Her sisters in the meantime stared at the peanut bar, the ice cream, the lollipop, and forgot entirely how miserable and frightened they had been only a few moments ago.

"Where'd you get all that?" demanded Ella.

"Oh, the policeman got them for me. He was awful nice. They're all nice around here. Want some?" She generously held out the peanut bar.

Mama thanked the policemen and then hustled her brood out. "From now on until we reach home," Mama said to Henny, "you'll stay beside me with your hand in mine. You're not going to get lost again today."

On the way to the streetcar, Henny told them all that had happened. She had been so interested in the freak show that she had not noticed the others leaving. She, Ella, and Sarah had dropped hands long before then so she just took it for granted that they were near. The barker had brought out another marvel — a midget, the tiniest lady she had ever seen. "Why even Gertie is a giant compared to her!" Henny said. She had stared and stared completely unaware of the passing of time. She thought that if she waited long enough some new freak would be shown. But nobody else was brought out, and she grew tired of standing still for so long. Only then did she think to look around her and discovered that Mama and her sisters had gone ahead without her. She walked on a little, looking for them.

"Weren't you scared?" asked Sarah.

"Nah — I knew I'd get found," boasted Henny.

She had stopped to look at the marvelous sights, even forgetting now and then that she was alone. She passed a policeman and that reminded her that policemen took care of lost children in the city. Perhaps policemen in Coney Island took care of them too. So she had walked over and said simply, "I'm lost."

He had smiled down at her and said (Henny imitated the accent of the policeman), "Air ye now! Well, ye come along with me and I'll take ye to where mamas always look for their lost little ones."

He had taken her by the hand and together they walked to the police station. On the way he had stopped and bought her the peanut bar and lollipop.

"The captain at the station house wanted to buy ice-cream cones for all the children," continued Henny, "but they all just sat there and cried and cried and said they wanted nothing but their Mamas. So he bought only one cone — for me. I wish he had bought some for the others also. Then they could have given them to me if they didn't feel like eating them."

By this time four other little girls wished that they had been lost too.

When they got home, Papa was waiting at the station, his face anxious and unhappy. But the worry soon changed to relief when he caught sight of the family. "What made you so late?" he asked as soon as they got out of the car. All talked at once while Mama surrendered the sleeping Gertie into Papa's strong arms. On the way to the house, the story was told.

Papa looked sternly at Henny, shook his head, but said nothing. To Mama he said, "What a time you must have had."

Succos

SEPTEMBER WAS ALMOST OVER. The High Holy Days had come and gone. Rosh Hashana, the Jewish New Year, had been heralded with the blowing of the ram's horn in the synagogue; ten days later Yom Kippur, the Day of Atonement, had been honored with fasting and prayer. There was still another holiday on the calendar which would be celebrated before Jewish folk could once more settle down to a spell of ordinary living.

"My goodness," declared Sarah one day as the children were discussing the coming of Succos, "the Jewish holidays certainly come in bunches."

Succos is a thanksgiving for the harvest, lasting nine days.

A part of each of these days is spent in a specially built wooden hut which is known as a Succah. This is to recall the forefathers who had to dwell in wooden huts during their wanderings in the desert after they had left Egypt. The Succah might be built by each family or put up by the local synagogue. In the crowded sections of the lower East Side, there was not much space for any additional building so many families had to do their celebrating in the Succah built by the congregation. For Mama's family, however, the tiny backyard offered a good chance to celebrate at home.

Preparations for the building had been under way for some time. Even before Yom Kippur, Papa had begun to gather broad planks of wood which he stacked in piles in the backyard. The children had watched the piles grow higher each day. "Soon, soon," they kept telling one another, "Papa will begin building." But it wasn't until the day after Yom Kippur that the "soon" became "today."

At lunch Papa said, "I'll close the shop at three today so that I can start work on our Succah."

"Oh, Papa, may we watch you? May we, Papa?" the children clamored excitedly.

"Watch me!" replied Papa. "I should say not!"

Such unhappy looks as appeared on the children's faces! But Papa was only teasing. They soon saw that, for his eyes crinkled merrily in their corners as they always did when he was getting ready to smile. "Watch me, indeed! You'll have to help. I can't do it all by myself."

The children raced home from school that afternoon. Papa was already hard at work in the back yard. Schoolbooks were flung down, afternoon snacks were gobbled up, so eager were they to begin. When the gang of little girls descended upon him, Papa began to issue orders like a master carpenter. Such sawing and hammering and wiggle-wagging of tongues as went on in Mama's backyard! Mama had to shut the kitchen window to keep out the noise. But the children revelled in it. It was amazing how quickly a tiny wooden house could be put together when everybody helped. By the time Mama called them in for supper, one long and one short wall stood stoutly.

"Well, girls," Papa said, finally, "we'll have to stop now. We'll work some more tomorrow."

At the supper table Sarah said, "You know, Mama, I was telling the library lady about the Succah we're building. She said she never saw a Succah in her whole life! I wish she could see ours."

"Then why don't you invite her?" suggested Mama.

"Can I, Mama? Really? Do you think she'd come?"

"Why not? You can ask her tomorrow."

Everybody thought it was a wonderful idea. "When should she come?" asked Ella. "We don't want her to see the Succah until it's all finished."

"Let me see," said Mama. "Succos eve would be the best time. That's three days from now. The children's room at the library closes early and she can come right over. Now when you speak to her tomorrow, Sarah, be sure and say that your Mama and Papa would be very pleased if she would come."

The next afternoon when Sarah joined her sisters in the backyard, her face was glowing and she bubbled over with the news. "She's coming! The library lady's coming to our house on Succos eve! I'm so happy!" and she twirled and turned about the yard.

"Fine, Sarah," said Papa, "but if you want her to see a finished Succah, you'd better get to work."

One more day and the little house was finished. The walls of the Succah had been built of planks laid tightly one against the other, but the roof had only a few planks of wood widely spaced so that broad patches of sky came through. Ever since

Papa had built the roof, Gertie had wondered about that. She hadn't said anything because she supposed that it would be finished sooner or later, but here they were already working on the furnishings, and still the roof remained as unfinished as ever. "Papa," she said finally, "what kind of a funny ceiling is that?"

"Exactly the right kind for a Succah," Ella explained. "Papa will spread fresh green branches across the planks of wood and it will be the loveliest ceiling anyone could possibly want. Sparse enough so that the sun can shine through in the daytime and the stars peep in at night."

Papa nodded approvingly.

"Isn't it nice building the house you're going to live in?" Sarah said earnestly.

"Oh, I wish we could live in it for ever and ever!" added Charlotte.

"I hardly think you'd be comfortable in this Succah for ever and ever," Papa said. "But I know just how you feel. It *is* nice to be making with your own hands the thing you are going to use. I'll tell you what we'll do. We'll leave the little house up for about a month after the holiday so you can enjoy it."

"Oh, Papa," the children all cried, "how wonderful!"

"We can bring our doll dishes out here and play house, really and truly," Charlotte said.

"We can invite our friends over," added Ella.

"Why, we can use it in a million different ways," continued Sarah.

"And to think it'll be all ours for a whole month," Henny exulted.

"The darling, darling, little house!" Gertie said.

Building over for the day, the family came back into the kitchen once more.

"Well," Mama asked, "how are you getting along?"

"We're almost finished," everybody answered at once.

"Fine," Mama said. "What about the decorations? You know there's only one more day before the holiday begins."

Everybody looked at Ella. Decoration of the Succah was Ella's special job. The others helped, of course, but she was always the designer. Under Ella's direction the children cut different fruits from cardboard and colored them. They made strings of colored paper chains and crepe-paper flowers.

When they were all made, the children tacked the paper fruits on the walls. Charlie had come over; he strung the bright-colored chains across each other under the roof planks.

The paper flowers were arranged in Mama's cut-glass bowl and when it graced the Succah table, the little house looked festive indeed. The children were enchanted with it.

"Mama!" they called. "You must come out to see it!"

Mama came and admired. "It *is* lovely! I think it's the loveliest Succah we've ever had."

"You girls have done a wonderful job," Charlie praised them.

"I just can't wait till the library lady sees it," said Sarah. "What time is it, Papa?"

"A little after six. She'll be here any minute. You'd better meet her outside. She won't know where the backyard is."

Sarah skipped out joyously. Soon the sound of gay laughter could be heard and she reappeared, leading the smiling Miss Allen by the hand.

Suddenly Miss Allen stopped. Her laughter stopped too; her face grew pale and her eyes grew big.

The children looked at her in astonishment and then their gaze followed hers — straight across the yard to Charlie.

"Herbert!" the library lady whispered.

The children knew something was happening, something big. They could feel it. They looked at Mama to see if she understood. But Mama was just as surprised as they were, and so was Papa.

Charlie too seemed to have forgotten where he was. He walked towards the library lady. The yard was still. It was almost as if these two were the only ones alive in it. He took the girl's hands in both of his. "Kathy, Kathy!" he said brokenly. "I had begun to believe you were dead!"

Miss Allen started to laugh, only this time the laugh sounded more as if she were crying. "Oh, I'm very much alive, Herbert."

Sarah spoke up. "His name is Charlie."

For a fleeting moment, Ella felt again the pain of that night when Papa had first told her about Charlie. Was it really only two months ago?

"Herbert is his first name," she told the others. "Charlie is his middle name."

Charlie and Kathy just looked at each other.

"Aren't you going to kiss her?" cried Henny.

"Quiet!" Papa said sternly.

Charlie put his hands around Kathy's face, then bent down and kissed her. It was a wonderful moment.

Kathy looked up at Charlie. There were tears in her eyes

as she said, "Oh, my dear, I'm so glad you found me!"

"It was really the children who found you," Charlie said with a radiant face. He turned and looked at the silent group around them. "Thank you, you wonderful family — thank you for Kathy and me."

"I think you can thank yourselves, too," Mama said. "Is it likely that you would have met here tonight if each of you had not been a kind good friend to this family?"

Before Papa left for the synagogue, Mama brought out her shiny brass candlesticks with the holiday candles already in them. Placing them on the Succah table, she lit them and recited a prayer. With the soft candlelight spread through the wooden hut and the smell of the green branches on the roof planks, the place seemed heavenly to the children who sat there awaiting Papa's return.

"I can't stop thinking about Charlie and the library lady," said Sarah.

"To think that Charlie's lost sweetheart should be our own library lady," Charlotte added dreamily.

"It's just like a storybook come true," added Sarah.

"Why didn't they stay to eat?" Henny asked.

"Kathy wanted to go straight to Charlie's parents and make up with them. I was glad that she felt that way," Mama said. "I know Charlie was glad, too. They promised to come to see us very soon."

Papa had returned. As Mama passed the dishes through the kitchen window, the girls placed them on the Succah table.

"It's fun seeing the dishes come through the window," Ella said. "You can almost imagine that the food is being whisked out of the air and served by magic hands."

She moved one arm in a swinging gesture to illustrate her words. At the end of the swing, she suddenly found a platter of gefüllte fish in her hand.

"This fish was whisked right out of the icebox," Mama said. "Mind you don't drop it, or magic hands will be laid on you."

Everyone laughed as Ella set the fish down with great care. Next out the window came a large soup tureen filled with good hot chicken soup. Inside the tureen floated a Succos delicacy — kreplech (meat-filled dumplings). Then out the window came a covered bowl of vegetables. Next came a platter of chicken.

And last of all, but not out the window, came Mama.

A New Charlie

SOMETHING IMPORTANT WAS TAKING PLACE in Mama's house on this particular night. It was way past ten o'clock. That should have meant darkened rooms in which seven people lay sleeping peacefully. Tonight, however, lights shone in all the rooms, and everybody was still awake.

Mama was in bed but not in her bedroom. Both bed and Mama had been moved into the front room. The door of this room was shut tight so that the children could not see her. But she was not asleep. The children were all in bed but they were not asleep. Papa was prowling about the kitchen so, of course, he was not asleep either.

The children talked together in excited whispers. They

grew quiet only in those moments when a grownup walked through their bedroom on the way to and from the front room.

Papa was walking back and forth, back and forth across the kitchen floor. The children could hear his heavy steps mingled with the lighter, quicker steps of Tanta, and his voice was pitched low as he talked.

Who was Tanta? Why, Tanta was just Tanta. All of the other aunts could be called Tanta Rivka, Tanta Leah, Tanta Frieda, or Tanta Fannie, but not this Tanta. She had a name — it was Minnie — but the children never thought of using it. She was Tanta — *the Tanta* — for she was always on hand when Mama needed her. She was Mama's widowed sister and earned her own living by working in a factory, but she was ever ready to give up her job when she was needed. And she certainly was needed now!

Somebody else was in the house tonight — somebody the children knew very well, but tonight he was in an unfamiliar role. It was Doctor Fuchs, and he was paying no attention whatever to the children. In fact, he was not even paying any attention to Mama, who was his patient. He just lay in his shirt sleeves on a cot in the far bedroom which usually held Mama's bed. The cot had been set up especially for him, the children knew that — but why? Why was he resting? Why wasn't he doing something to make Mama's new baby come quickly?

Yes, a new baby was coming to join Mama's large family! There hadn't been a new baby in five years. The children were delighted at the prospect; that is — four of them were delighted. Gertie was not so sure. As a matter of fact, she had felt a funny lump in her throat all day, a sort of wanting-to-cry lump. She didn't exactly know why, but she had a feeling it had something to do with the coming of that new baby.

"I think six children will be ever so much nicer than five," Ella whispered. "Things can be divided evenly among six."

"I wonder what Mama will call her," Henny said.

"Her!" exclaimed Sarah. "What makes you so sure it will be a her!"

Henny answered, "Oh, Mama always has hers."

"Well, I, for one, am glad," Charlotte added loyally. "I think boys are horrid, anyway — always wanting to fight and throw each other around. When I get married and have children, I'm going to have only girl babies."

"Oh, you silly!" Henny told her. "You can't order your babies. You've got to take what you get."

"Well, I'm sure God will give me just what I want," replied Charlotte. "I'll just want girls so hard, He won't even be able to think about boys."

At this point, Tanta walked through the room, a cup of tea in her hand. The children stopped talking. She passed right by their beds, past Doctor Fuchs on the cot, and into the front room shutting the door firmly behind her. How the children wished they had magic eyes to see right through that door!

Henny began to giggle. "Doctor Fuchs certainly looks funny without his jacket on, doesn't he. He's got such a round, fat tummy and look at the way it moves up and down when he snores."

"What's he sleeping on the cot for?" Sarah asked. "Why doesn't he go into the front room to be with Mama?"

Ella answered her. "I heard him tell Tanta that it would be some time before the baby arrived so he's resting in the meantime."

"What's he resting for?" demanded Henny. "You'd think he was having the baby."

"I guess he's tired," Ella said. "There's no sense just sitting around waiting. It's late, you know."

Tanta was coming out of the front room again. Ella called to her softly.

"Aren't you children asleep yet?" Tanta said. "Mama wouldn't like that. Now if you will go right to sleep, I promise to awaken you the very minute the baby is born." She went about tucking them in.

The children really tried to sleep, but there were so many distractions. Papa talked; the gaslight flickered in the children's bedroom; Doctor Fuchs snored gently on the cot in the adjoining room; and occasionally Mama called from the front room.

Gertie was tossing about restlessly. She had said not a word for a long time, because the lump in her throat was so big. Presently it worked its way up to her eyes and changed into salty tears that trickled slowly down her cheeks. Without her wanting it to happen, a sob broke through, and then another, and still another.

"Why, Gertie," Charlotte asked in surprise, "what's the matter?"

All the tight, hurt feelings inside of her, the confusion and jealousy, were suddenly poured out in a rush of words. "I don't want Mama to have another baby," Gertie cried. "I'm the baby! I'm the baby!"

The others sat up in their beds.

"Hush," Ella commanded. "Not so loud. You wouldn't want Mama to hear you."

Gertie buried her face in her pillow. Of course she didn't want Mama to hear her. She hadn't wanted anyone to hear her, but it was too late now.

Sarah said, "I suppose that's the way you feel when you've been the baby as long as Gertie. Nobody else in this family ever had the chance to feel like that. Another little sister always came along while we were still babies ourselves."

"That's so," agreed Ella. "But what Gertie doesn't understand is that it's really nicer being an older sister. For instance, being an older sister means that you can take care of the baby. Remember it will be helpless, and it will need you. It doesn't mean that people will love *you* any less — it's just that you will be more important, more grown-up. You will be closer to the rest of us, but the baby will be all alone, really, because it will not have anybody close to its own age as we have each other."

Gertie lay still. Her sobbing grew quieter. The sisters looked at one another but said nothing. They had to give Gertie time to get used to the idea of being an older sister. In a few minutes the sobbing stopped altogether, and the exhausted little girl was asleep.

Charlotte's eyes winked and blinked. She even put her fingers in her mouth, wetting them, and drew them across her eyelids in her attempts to stay awake. But it did not help her for long. She too fell fast asleep.

Henny tossed and turned until she finally slept. That left only Ella and Sarah still awake.

"Why don't you lie down on the couch awhile?" Tanta was saying to Papa in the kitchen. "You've been through this often enough not to be so impatient. You don't even have to worry about what it'll be. You know it'll be another girl."

"I know," Papa answered. "I know, but there's always the hope. Maybe this time it'll be a son. A son — to carry on my name, to go to the synagogue with me — oh, what's the use even thinking about it. It's sure to be another daughter. I'll do as you say. I'll lie down for a minute."

Ella and Sarah looked at each other. They had heard. "My," murmured Sarah, "Papa certainly wants a boy child, doesn't he?"

As the night wore on, two more little girls joined their sisters in dreamland.

In the early morning hours, Ella suddenly opened her eyes with the feeling that something important was happening. The baby, she thought at once! It must have come! She sat up quickly, but nothing seemed changed. Papa was still walking back and forth in the kitchen. And the doctor — she looked through the heavy portieres separating the bedrooms. The doctor was not there! And where was Tanta? Tanta and the doctor must be with Mama. And then she heard it — the thin wailing of a baby. It had come at last! Oh, what was it? What was it?

From the kitchen the walking sounds had stopped. Papa had heard the wailing too. A kitchen chair scraped across the floor. Papa must have sat down. When she leaned way out of bed, she could just see him. He was sitting with his elbows resting on the kitchen table, his head cupped in his hands — waiting.

Then the front-room door opened. Tanta came out, a small blanketed bundle held tight in her arms. Her face was wreathed in smiles as she passed Ella and went on to the kitchen — to the waiting father.

"You've got what you wanted at last," she cried out happily, "a son, a son!"

183

Papa merely stared at her unbelievingly.

"Well, don't you want to look at your son?" Tanta asked, holding out the precious bundle. Papa made no attempt to touch the new baby. He just sat still, then covered his face with his hands, and to Ella's amazement, his shoulders began to heave as if — as if he were crying. Ella couldn't believe it. Papa wouldn't cry; Papa never cried. Besides, what was there to cry about? Still the choking sounds Papa was making certainly couldn't be laughter.

Ella slipped out of bed and hurried into the kitchen. She put her arm about her father's shoulders and said wonderingly, "Why are you crying? Aren't you glad it's a boy? You were so anxious to have a son."

Papa took a handkerchief out of his pocket, wiped his eyes and blew his nose vigorously. Then he turned a shining, smiling face to Ella. "I was crying with happiness, dear child. Come, let's look at him together." He took Ella's hand in his and they both peeked at the rosy infant sleeping in Tanta's arms.

Meanwhile Doctor Fuchs had come into the kitchen looking once more his dignified self now that he had his coat on again. "Congratulations," he said to Papa. "And what are you doing up at this hour, young lady? Had to see your baby brother, eh? Well, and now that you have seen him, what do you think of him?"

"His face is so red, Doctor," Ella said, "almost as if he had scarlet fever."

The doctor laughed. "You needn't worry about his face. It'll be the normal color soon enough. Tanta, you'd better put him back in his cradle and be very quiet about it. His mother

is sleeping, and I don't want her disturbed." He slapped Papa on the back. "All right, I'll come back later in the day. Good-by now." And he was gone.

Tanta put the baby to bed while Papa sank contentedly on the couch to enjoy the first real sleep that night. The cot the doctor had used was remade for Tanta, and she too was soon asleep. Ella crawled back into her own bed and snuggled up against Sarah's warm body. She was bursting with the news. If only she could awaken the others and tell them now. But Papa had asked her to wait until morning because their excitement would prevent anyone's sleeping.

Ella was sure she would not be able to fall asleep, but she did. When next she opened her eyes, it was only to discover that someone else had had the pleasure of telling the wonderful news. She was disappointed but not for long.

"Why didn't you wake us up as soon as it happened, you old meany?" Henny asked.

"Yes, you knew hours before we did. That wasn't fair!" Charlotte was indignant.

"I wanted to," Ella defended herself, "only Papa and Tanta wouldn't let me. They said I had to wait until morning. What difference does it make? You know now. Have you seen him? How is Mama? Is she awake? Can we see her?"

"Yes, she's awake. As soon as you get out of bed, we'll be able to go in." The children were so excited. "Hurry up!"

The five little girls tiptoed into the front room. They smiled at Mama, and she smiled back at them. She motioned with her hand to the cradle and at once they surrounded the sleeping baby to admire and exclaim, "Isn't he sweet?" They gently touched the baby face. "How soft his skin is!" "Look at the cunning hands." "He's a darling!" "I'd just love to hold him."

They would have remained there forever but Papa came in to shoo them out. "Mama needs rest," he cautioned. "Better run along and get dressed. Tanta will need your help."

"What are we going to name him?" Ella asked, looking adoringly at her baby brother.

"We will have to talk about that," Papa said. "I thought we might name him after my grandfather Chaim, if Mama is willing — and then we would have a new Charlie."

Mama said, "Why, that's a wonderful thought, Papa! That's a name we all love."

"Little Charlie," Gertie murmured lovingly, looking down at him. She seemed to have accepted the idea of being a big sister.

"You know," Charlotte spoke up, "it'll seem awful funny to see a little child in boy's clothes in this house."

"He's lucky," Henny added. "He won't have to wear hand-me-down clothes like the rest of us. He'll always be getting new clothes."

"Do you think he'll like to play with dolls?" Gertie asked.

"Silly!" answered Henny. "Boys don't play with dolls. They like fire engines, and soldiers, and things like that. That means he'll be getting new toys too."

"No matter what it's going to be like, it'll be all right with me," said Ella. "But we aren't an all-of-a-kind family any more."

"In a way we are," Mama said, smiling. "I think that means more than our having five daughters. It means we're all close and loving and loyal — and our family will always be that."

Everyone agreed. Even baby Charlie opened his mouth as if he were about to speak. But it was only a yawn.